William Shakespeare

Shakespeare's Sonnets

Reproduced in Facsimile from the Unrivalled Original in the Library....

William Shakespeare

Shakespeare´s Sonnets
Reproduced in Facsimile from the Unrivalled Original in the Library....

ISBN/EAN: 9783337142599

Printed in Europe, USA, Canada, Australia, Japan

Cover: Foto ©Andreas Hilbeck / pixelio.de

More available books at **www.hansebooks.com**

SONNETS;

REPRODUCED IN FACSIMILE BY

THE NEW PROCESS OF PHOTO-ZINCOGRAPHY

IN USE AT

HER MAJESTY'S ORDNANCE SURVEY OFFICE

From the unrivalled Original in the Library of Bridgewater
House, by Permission of the Right Hon. the
Earl of Ellesmere.

LONDON

LOVELL REEVE & CO., HENRIETTA STREET, COVENT G

1862.

SHAKE-SPEARES

SONNETS.

Neuer before Imprinted.

———————————

———————————

AT LONDON
By G. Eld for T. T. and are
to be folde by william Apley.
1609.

TO. THE. ONLIE. BEGETTER. OF.
THESE. INSVING. SONNETS.
Mr. W. H. ALL. HAPPINESSE.
AND. THAT. ETERNITIE.
PROMISED.

BY.

OVR. EVER-LIVING. POET.

WISHETH.

THE. WELL-WISHING.
ADVENTVRER. IN.
SETTING.
FORTH.

T. T.

SHAKE-SPEARES,
SONNETS.

FRom fairest creatures we defire increafe,
　That thereby beauties *Rofe* might neuer die,
But as the riper fhould by time deceafe,
His tender heire might beare his memory:
But thou contracted to thine owne bright eyes,
Feed'ft thy lights flame with felfe fubftantiall fewell,
Making a famine where aboundance lies,
Thy felfe thy foe,to thy fweet felfe too cruell:
Thou that art now the worlds frefh ornament,
And only herauld to the gaudy fpring,
Within thine owne bud burieft thy content,
And tender chorle makft waft in niggarding:
　　Pitty the world,or elfe this glutton be,
　　To eate the worlds due,by the graue and thee.

2

VVHen fortie Winters fnall befeige thy brow,
　　And digge deep trenches in thy beauties field,
Thy youthes proud liuery fo gaz'd on now,
Wil be a totter'd weed of fmal worth heid:
Then being askt,where all thy beautie lies,
Where all the treafure of thy lufty daies;
To fay within thine owne deepe funken eyes,
Were an all-eating fhame,and thriftleffe praife.
How much more praife deferu'd thy beauties vfe,
If thou couldft anfwere this faire child of mine
Shall fum my count,and make my old excufe
Proouing his beautie by fucceffion thine.

This were to be new made when thou art ould,
And fee thy blood warme when thou feel'ft it could,

3

Ooke in thy glaffe and tell the face thou vewest,
Now is the time that face fhould forme an other,
Whofe frefh repaire if now thou not renewest,
Thou dooft beguile the world, vnbleffe fome mother.
For where is fhe fo faire whofe vn-eard wombe
Difdaines the tillage of thy husbandry?
Or who is he fo fond will be the tombe,
Of his felfe loue to ftop pofterity?
Thou art thy mothers glaffe and fhe in thee
Calls backe the louely Aprill of her prime,
So thou through windowes of thine age fhalt fee,
Difpight of wrinkles this thy goulden time.
    But if thou liue remembred not to be,
    Die fingle and thine Image dies with thee.

4

Nthrifty louelineffe why doft thou fpend,
Vpon thy felfe thy beauties legacy?
Natures bequeft giues nothing but doth lend,
And being franck fhe lends to thofe are free:
Then beautious nigard why dooft thou abufe,
The bountious largeffe giuen thee to giue?
Profitles vferer why dooft thou vfe
So great a fumme of fummes yet can'ft not liue?
For hauing traffike with thy felfe alone,
Thou of thy felfe thy fweet felfe doft deceaue,
Then how when nature calls thee to be gone,
What acceptable *Audit* can'ft thou leaue?
    Thy vnuf'd beauty muft be tomb'd with thee,
    Which vfed liues th'executor to be.

5

Hofe howers that with gentle worke did frame,
The louely gaze where euery eye doth dwell
Will play the tirants to the very fame,

And

And that vnfaire which fairely doth excell:
For neuer resting time leads Summer on,
To hidious winter and confounds him there,
Sap checkt with frost and lustie leau's quite gon.
Beauty ore-snow'd and barenes euery where,
Then were not summers distillation left:
A liquid prisoner pent in walls of glasse,
Beauties effect with beauty were bereft,
Nor it nor noe remembrance what it was.
　　But flowers distil'd though they with winter meete,
　　Leese but their show, their substance still liues sweet.

6

THen let not winters wragged hand deface,
　In thee thy summer ere thou be distil'd:
Make sweet some viall; treasure thou some place,
With beauties treasure ere it be selfe kil'd:
That vse is not forbidden vsery,
Which happies those that pay the willing lone;
That's for thy selfe to breed an other thee,
Or ten times happier be it ten for one,
Ten times thy selfe were happier then thou art,
If ten of thine ten times refigur'd thee,
Then what could death doe if thou should'st depart,
Leauing thee liuing in posterity?
　　Be not selfe-wild for thou art much too faire,
　　To be deaths conquest and make wormes thine heire.

7

LOe in the Orient when the gracious light.
　Lifts vp his burning head, each vnder eye
Doth homage to his new appearing sight,
Seruing with lookes his sacred maiesty,
And hauing climb'd the steepe vp heauenly hill,
Resembling strong youth in his middle age,
Yet mortall lookes adore his beauty still,
Attending on his goulden pilgrimage:
But when from high-most pich with wery car,

Like feeble age he reeleth from the day,
The eyes(fore dutious)now conuerted are
From his low tract and looke an other way:
   So thou,thy selfe out-going in thy noon:
   Vnlok'd on dieft vnleffe thou get a fonne.

8

MVfick to heare,why hear'ft thou mufick fadly,
  Sweets with fweets warre not ,ioy delights in ioy:
Why lou'ft thou that which thou receauft not gladly,
Or elfe receau'ft with pleafure thine annoy ?
If the true concord of well tuned founds,
By vnions married do offend thine eare,
They do but fweetly chide thee, who confounds
In fingleneffe the parts that thou fhould'ft beare:
Marke how one ftring fweet husband to an other,
Strikes each in each by mutuall ordering;
Refembling fier,and child, and happy mother,
Who all in one,one pleafing note do fing:
   Whofe fpeechleffe fong being many,feeming one,
   Sings this to thee thou fingle wilt proue none.

9.

IS it for feare to wet a widdowes eye,
  That thou confum'ft thy felfe in fingle life?
Ah;if thou iffuleffe fhalt hap to die,
The world will waile thee like a makeleffe wife,
The world wilbe thy widdow and ftill weepe,
That thou no forme of thee haft left behind,
When euery priuat widdow well may keepe,
By childrens eyes,her husbands fhape in minde:
Looke what an vnthrift in the world doth fpend
Shifts but his place,for ftill the world inioyes it
But beauties wafte hath in the world an end,
And kept vnvfde the vfer fo deftroyes it:
   No loue toward others in that bofome fits
   That on himfelfe fuch murdrous fhame comnits.

10

FOr shame deny that thou bear'ft loue to any
Who for thy felfe art fo vnprouident
Graunt if thou wilt,thou art belou'd of many,
But that thou none lou'ft is moft euident:
For thou art fo poffeft with murdrous hate,
That gainft thy felfe thou ftickft not to confpire,
Seeking that beautious roofe to ruinate
Which to repaire fhould be thy chiefe defire :
O change thy thought,that I may change my minde,
Shall hate be fairer log'd then gentle loue?
Be as thy prefence is gracious and kind,
Or to thy felfe at leaft kind harted proue,
     Make thee an other felfe for loue of me,
     That beauty ftill may liue in thine or thee.

11

AS faft as thou fhalt wane fo faft thou grow'ft,
In one of thine,from that which thou departeft,
And that frefh bloud which yongly thou beftow'ft,
Thou maift call thine,when thou from youth conuerteft,
Herein liues wifdome,beauty,and increafe,
Without this follie,age,and could decay,
If all were minded fo,the times fhould ceafe,
And threefcoore yeare would make the world away:
Let thofe whom nature hath not made for ftore,
Harfh,featureleffe,and rude , barrenly perrifh,
Looke whom fhe beft indow'd,fhe gaue the more;
Which bountious guift thou fhouldft in bounty cherrifh,
     She caru'd thee for her feale,and ment therby,
     Thou fhouldft print more,not let that coppy die.

12

VVHen I doe count the clock that tels the time,
     And fee the braue day funck in hidious night,
When I behold the violet paft prime,
And fable curls or filuer'd ore with white :
When lofty trees I fee barren of leaues,
Which erft from heat did canopie the herd

And

And Sommers greene all girded vp in sheaues
Borne on the beare with white and bristly beard:
Then of thy beauty do I question make
That thou among the wastes of time must goe,
Since sweets and beauties do them-selues forsake,
  And die as fast as they see others grow,
    And nothing gainst Times sieth can make defence
    Saue breed to braue him, when he takes thee hence.

13

O That you were your selfe, but loue you are
  No longer yours, then you your selfe here liue,
Against this cumming end you should prepare,
And your sweet semblance to some other giue.
So should that beauty which you hold in lease
Find no determination, then you were
You selfe again after your selfes decease,
When your sweet issue your sweet forme should beare.
Who lets so faire a house fall to decay,
Which husbandry in honour might vphold,
Against the stormy gusts of winters day
And barren rage of deaths eternall cold?
    O none but vnthrifts, deare my loue you know,
    You had a Father, let your Son say so.

14

NOt from the stars do I my iudgement plucke,
  And yet me thinkes I haue Astronomy,
But not to tell of good, or euil lucke,
Of plagues, of dearths, or seasons quallity,
Nor can I fortune to breefe mynuits tell;
Pointing to each his thunder, raine and winde,
Or say with Princes if it shal go wel
By oft predict that I in heauen finde.
But from thine eies my knowledge I deriue,
And constant stars in them I read such art
As truth and beautie shal together thriue
If from thy selfe, to store thou wouldst conuert:

Or

Or elſe of thee this I prognoſticate,
Thy end is Truthes and Beauties doome and date.

15

WHen I conſider euery thing that growes
Holds in perfeſtion but a little moment.
That this huge ſtage preſenteth nought but ſhowes
Whereon the Stars in ſecret influence comment.
When I perceiue that men as plants increaſe,
Cheared and checkt euen by the ſelfe-ſame skie:
Vaunt in their youthfull ſap, at height decreaſe,
And were their braue ſtate out of memory.
Then the conceit of this inconſtant ſtay,
Sets you moſt rich in youth before my ſight,
Where waſtfull time debateth with decay
To change your day of youth to ſullied night,
  And all in war with Time for loue of you
  As he takes from you, I ingraft you new.

16

BVt wherefore do not you a mightier waie
Make warre vppon this bloudie tirant time? ;
And fortifie your ſelfe in your decay
With meanes more bleſſed then my barren rime?
Now ſtand you on the top of happie houres,
And many maiden gardens yet vnſet,
With vertuous wiſh would beare your liuing flowers,
Much liker then your painted counterfeit:
So ſhould the lines of life that life repaire
Which this (Times penſel or my pupill pen)
Neither in inward worth nor outward faire
Can make you liue your ſelfe in eies of men,
  To giue away your ſelfe, keeps your ſelfe ſtill,
  And you muſt liue drawne by your owne ſweet skill,

17

VVHo will beleeue my verſe in time to come
If it were fild with your moſt high deſerts?

B 4   Though

Though yet heauen knowes it is but as a tombe
Which hides your life, and shewes not halfe your parts:
If I could write the beauty of your eyes,
And in fresh numbers number all your graces,
The age to come would say this Poet lies,
Such heauenly touches nere toucht earthly faces.
So should my papers (yellowed with their age)
Be scorn'd,like old men of lesse truth then tongue,
And your true rights be termd a Poets rage,
And stretched miter of an Antique song.
   But were some childe of yours aliue that time,
   You should liue twise in it,and in my rime.

18.

SHall I compare thee to a Summers day?
  Thou art more louely and more temperate:
Rough windes do shake the darling buds of Maie,
And Sommers leafe hath all too short a date:
Sometime too hot the eye of heauen shines,
And often is his gold complexion dimm'd,
And euery faire from faire some-time declines,
By chance,or natures changing course vntrim'd:
But thy eternall Sommer shall not fade,
Nor loose possession of that faire thou ow'st,
Nor shall death brag thou wandr'st in his shade,
When in eternall lines to time thou grow'st,
   So long as men can breath or eyes can see,
   So long liues this,and this giues life to thee,

19

DEuouring time blunt thou the Lyons pawes,
  And make the earth deuoure her owne sweet brood,
Plucke the keene teeth from the fierce Tygers yawes,
And burne the long liu'd Phœnix in her blood,
Make glad and sorry seasons as thou fleet'st,
And do what ere thou wilt swift-footed time
To the wide world and all her fading sweets:
But I forbid thee one most heinous crime,

C

O carue not with thy howers my loues faire brow,
Nor draw noe lines there with thine antique pen,
Him in thy courſe vntainted doe allow,
For beauties patterne to ſucceding men.
  Yet doe thy worſt ould Time diſpight thy wrong,
  My loue ſhall in my verſe euer liue young.

20

A Womans face with natures owne hand painted,
  Haſte thou the Maſter Miſtris of my paſſion,
A womans gentle hart but not acquainted
With ſhifting change as is falſe womens faſhion,
An eye more bright then theirs, leſſe falſe in rowling:
Gilding the obiect where-vpon it gazeth,
A man in hew all *Hews* in his controwling,
Which ſteales mens eyes and womens ſoules amaſeth,
And for a woman wert thou firſt created,
Till nature as ſhe wrought thee fell a dotinge,
And by addition me of thee defeated,
By adding one thing to my purpoſe nothing.
  But ſince ſhe prickt thee out for womens pleaſure,
  Mine be thy loue and thy loues vſe their treaſure.

21

SO is it not with me as with that Muſe,
  Stird by a painted beauty to his verſe,
Who heauen it ſelfe for ornament doth vſe,
And euery faire with his faire doth reherſe,
Making a coopelment of proud compare
With Sunne and Moone, with earth and ſeas rich gems:
With Aprills firſt borne flowers and all things rare,
That heauens ayre in this huge rondure hems,
O let me true in loue but truly write,
And then beleeue me, my loue is as faire,
As any mothers childe, though not ſo bright
As thoſe gould candells fixt in heauens ayer:
  Let them ſay more that like of heare-ſay well,
  I will not prayſe that purpoſe not to ſell.

C

22

MY glasse shall not perswade me I am ould,
So long as youth and thou are of one date,
But when in thee times forrwes I behould,
Then look I death my daies should expiate.
For all that beauty that doth couer thee,
Is but the seemely rayment of my heart,
Which in thy brest doth liue,as thine in me,
How can I then be elder then thou art?
O therefore loue be of thy selfe so wary,
As I not for my selfe,but for thee will,
Bearing thy heart which I will keepe so chary
As tender nurse her babe from faring ill,
    Presume not on thy heart when mine is slaine,
    Thou gau'st me thine not to giue backe againe.

23

AS an vnperfect actor on the stage,
Who with his feare is put besides his part,
Or some fierce thing repleat with too much rage,
Whose strengths abondance weakens his owne heart;
So I for feare of truft,forget to say,
The perfect ceremony of loues right,
And in mine owne loues strength seeme to decay,
Ore-charg'd with burthen of mine owne loues might:
O let my books be then the eloquence,
And do nb presagers of my speaking brest,
Who pleade for loue,and look for recompence,
More then that tonge that more hath more exprest.
    O learne to read what silent loue hath writ,
    To heare wit eies belongs to loues fine wiht.

24

MIne eye hath play'd the painter and hath steeld,
Thy beauties forme in table of my heart,
My body is the frame wherein ti's held,
And perspectiue it is best Painters art.
For through the Painter must you see his skill,

To finde where your true Image pictur'd lies,
Which in my bofomes fhop is hanging ftil,
That hath his windowes glazed with thine eyes:
Now fee what good-turnes eyes for eies haue done,
Mine eyes haue drawne thy fhape, and thine for me
Are windowes to my breft, where-through the Sun
Delights to peepe, to gaze therein on thee
 Yet eyes this cunning want to grace their art
 They draw but what they fee, know not the hart.

25

Et thofe who are in fauor with their ftars,
 Of publike honour and proud titles boft,
Whilft I whome fortune of fuch tryumph bars
Vnlookt for ioy in that I honour moft;
Great Princes fauorites their faire leaues fpread,
But as the Marygold at the funs eye,
And in them-felues their pride lies buried,
For at a frowne they in their glory die.
The painefull warrier famofed for worth,
After a thoufand victories once foild,
Is from the booke of honour rafed quite,
And all the reft forgot for which he toild:
 Then happy I that loue and am beloued
 Where I may not remoue, nor be remoued.

26

Ord of my loue, to whome in vaffalage
 Thy merrit hath my dutie ftrongly knit;
To thee I fend this written ambaffage
To witneffe duty, not to fhew my wit.
Duty fo great, which wit fo poore as mine
May make feeme bare, in wanting words to fhew it;
But that I hope fome good conceipt of thine
In thy foules thought (all naked) will beftow it:
Til whatfoeuer ftar that guides my mouing,
Points on me gratioufly with faire afpect,
And puts apparrell on my tottered louing,

To

To show me worthy of their sweet respect,
   Then may I dare to boast how I doe loue thee,
   Til then,not show my head where thou maift proue me

27

WEary with toyle,I haft me to my bed,
   The deare repofe for lims with trauaill tired,
But then begins a iourny in my head
To worke my mind,when boddies work's expired.
For then my thoughts(from far where I abide)
Intend a zelous pilgrimage to thee,
And keepe my drooping eye-lids open wide,
Looking on darknes which the blind doe fee.
Saue that my foules imaginary fight
Prefents their fhaddoe to my fightles view,
Which like a iewell(hunge in gaftly night)
Makes blacke night beautious,and her old face new.
   Loe thus by day my lims,by night my mind,
   For thee,and for my felfe,noe quiet finde.

28

HOw can I then returne in happy plight
   That am debard the benifit of reft?
When daies oppreffion is not eazd by night,
But day by night and night by day opreft.
And each(though enimes to ethers raigne)
Doe in confent fhake hands to torture me,
The one by toyle,the other to complaine
How far I toyle,ftill farther off from thee.
I tell the Day to pleafe him thou art bright,
And do'ft him grace when clouds doe blot the heauen:
So flatter I the fwart complexiond night,
When fparkling ftars twire not thou guil'ft th' eauen.
   But day doth daily draw my forrowes longer,(ftronger
   And night doth nightly make greefes length feeme

29

WHen in difgrace with Fortune and mens eyes,
   I all alone beweepe my out-caft ftate,

And

And trouble deafe heauen with my bootlesse cries,
And looke vpon my selfe and curse my fate,
Wishing me like to one more rich in hope,
Featur'd like him, like him with friends possest,
Desiring this mans art, and that mans skope,
With what I most inioy contented least,
Yet in these thoughts my selfe almost despising,
Haplye I thinke on thee, and then my state,
(Like to the Larke at breake of daye arising)
From sullen earth sings himns at Heauens gate,
    For thy sweet loue remembred such welth brings,
    That then I skorne to change my state with Kings.

30

VVHen to the Sessions of sweet silent thought,
    I sommon vp remembrance of things past,
I sigh the lacke of many a thing I sought,
And with old woes new waile my deare times waste:
Then can I drowne an eye(vn-vs'd to flow)
For precious friends hid in deaths dateles night,
And weepe a fresh loues long since canceld woe,
And mone th'expence of many a vannisht sight.
Then can I greeue at greeuances fore-gon,
And heauily from woe to woe tell ore
The sad account of fore-bemoued mone,
Which I new pay as if not payd before.
    But if the while I thinke on thee (deare friend)
    All losses are restord, and sorrowes end.

31

Thy bosome is indeared with all hearts,
    Which I by lacking haue supposed dead,
And there raignes Loue and all Loues louing parts,
And all those friends which I thought buried.
How many a holy and obsequious teare
Hath deare religious loue stolne from mine eye,
As interest of the dead, which now appeare,
But things remou'd that hidden in there lie,

                       To

Thou art the graue where buried loue doth liue,
Hung with the tropheis of my louers gon,
Who all their parts of me to thee did giue,
That due of many, now is thine alone.
　　Their images I lou'd, I view in thee,
　　And thou(all they)haſt all the all of me.

32

IF thou ſuruiue my well contented daie,
When that churle death my bones with duſt ſhall couer
And ſhalt by fortune once more re-ſuruay:
Theſe poore rude lines of thy deceaſea Louer:
Compare them with the bett'ring of the time,
And though they be out-ſtript by euery pen,
Reſerue them for my loue, not for their rime,
Exceeded by the hight of happier men.
Oh then voutſafe me but this louing thought,
Had my friends Muſe growne with this growing age,
A dearer birth then this his loue had brought
To march in ranckes of better equipage:
　　But ſince he died and Poets better proue,
　　Theirs for their ſtile ile read, his for his loue.

33

FVll many a glorious morning haue I ſeene,
Flatter the mountaine tops with ſoueraine eie,
Kiſſing with golden face the meddowes greene;
Guilding pale ſtreames with heauenly alcumy:
Anon permit the baſeſt clouds to ride,
With ougly rack on his celeſtiall face,
And from the for-lorne world his viſage hide
Stealing vnſeene to weſt with this diſgrace:
Euen ſo my Sunne one early morne did ſhine,
With all triumphant ſplendor on my brow,
But out alack, he was but one houre mine,
The region cloude hath mask'd him from me now.
　　Yet him for this, my loue no whit diſdaineth,
　　Suns of the world may ſtaine, whē heauens ſun ſtainteh.

34

34

VVHy didſt thou promiſe ſuch a beautious day,
   And make me trauaile forth without my cloake,
To let baſe cloudes ore-take me in my way,
Hiding thy brau'ry in their rotten ſmoke.
Tis not enough that through the cloude thou breake,
To dry the raine on my ſtorme-beaten face,
For no man well of ſuch a ſalue can ſpeake,
That heales the wound, and cures not the diſgrace:
Nor can thy ſhame giue phiſicke to my griefe,
Though thou repent , yet I haue ſtill the loſſe,
Th'offenders ſorrow lends but weake reliefe
To him that beares the ſtrong offenſes loſſe.
   Ah but thoſe teares are pearle which thy loue ſheeds,
   And they are ritch,and ranſome all ill deeds.

35

NO more bee greeu'd at that which thou haſt done,
   Roſes haue thornes,and ſiluer fountaines mud,
Cloudes and eclipſes ſtaine both Moone and Sunne,
And loathſome canker liues in ſweeteſt bud.
All men make faults,and euen I in this,
Authorizing thy treſpas with compare,
My ſelfe corrupting ſaluing thy amiſſe,
Excuſing their ſins more then their ſins are:
For to thy ſenſuall fault I bring in ſence,
Thy aduerſe party is thy Aduocate,
And gainſt my ſelfe a lawfull plea commence,
Such ciuill war is in my loue and hate,
   That I an acceſſary needs muſt be,
   To that ſweet theefe which ſourely robs from me,

36

LEt me confeſſe that we two muſt be twaine,
   Although our vndeuided loues are one:
So ſhall thoſe blots that do with me remaine,
Without thy helpe , by me be borne alone.
In our two loues there is but one reſpect,

Though

Though in our liues a feperable fpight,
Which though it alter not loues fole effect,
Yet doth it fteale fweet houres from loues delight,
I may not euer-more acknowledge thee,
Leaft my bewailed guilt fhould do thee fhame,
Nor thou with publike kindneffe honour me,
Vnleffe thou take that honour from thy name:
    But doe not fo,I loue thee in fuch fort,
    As thou being mine,mine is thy good report.

37

AS a decrepit father takes delight,
  To fee his actiue childe do deeds of youth,
So I, made lame by Fortunes deareft fpight
Take all my comfort of thy worth and truth.
For whether beauty,birth,or wealth,or wit,
Or any of thefe all,or all,or more
Intitled in their parts,do crowned fit,
I make my loue ingrafted to this ftore:
So then I am not lame,poore, nor difpif'd,
Whilft that this fhadow doth fuch fubftance giue,
That I in thy abundance am fuffic'd,
And by a part of all thy glory liue:
    Looke what is beft,that beft I wifh in thee,
    This wifh I haue,then ten times happy me.

38

HOw can my Mufe want fubiect to inuent
  While thou doft breath that poor'ft into my verfe,
Thine owne fweet argument,to excellent,
For euery vulgar paper to rehearfe:
Oh giue thy felfe the thankes if ought in me,
Worthy perufal ftand againft thy fight,
For who's fo dumbe that cannot write to thee,
When thou thy felfe doft giue inuention light?
Be thou the tenth Mufe,ten times more in worth
Then thofe old nine which rimers inuocate,
And he that calls on thee,let him bring forth

Eternall

. Eternal numbers to out-liue long date.
　　If my flight Muse doe pleafe thefe curious daies,
　　The paine be mine, but thine fhal be the praife.

39

OH how thy worth with manners may I finge,
　　When thou art all the better part of me?
What can mine owne praife to mine owne feife bring;
And what is't but mine owne when I praife thee,
Euen for this, let vs deuided liue,
And our deare loue loofe name of fingle one,
That by this feperation I may giue:
That due to thee which thou deferu'ft alone:
Oh abfence what a torment wouldft thou proue,
Were it not thy foure leifure gaue fweet leaue,
To entertaine the time with thoughts of loue,
VVhich time and thoughts fo fweetly doft deceiue,
　　And that thou teacheft how to make one twaine,
　　By praifing him here who doth hence remaine.

40

TAke all my loues, my loue, yea take them all,
　　What haft thou then more then thou hadft before?
No loue, my loue, that thou maift true loue call,
All mine was thine, before thou hadft this more:
Then if for my loue, thou my loue receiueft,
I cannot blame thee, for my loue thou vieft,
But yet be blam'd, if thou this felfe deceaueft
By wilfull tafte of what thy felfe refufeft.
I doe forgiue thy robb'rie gentle theefe
Although thou fteale thee all my pouerty:
And yet loue knowes it is a greater griefe
To beare loues wrong, then hates knowne iniury.
　　Lafciuious grace, in whom all il wel fhowes,
　　Kill me with fpights yet we muft not be foes.

41

THofe pretty wrongs that liberty commits,
　　When I am fome-time abfent from thy heart,

D　　　　　　　　　　　　　　　　　　　Thy

Thy beautie,and thy yeares full well befits,
For still temptacion followes where thou art.
Gentle thou art,and therefore to be wonne,
Beautious thou art,therefore to be assailed.
And when a woman woes,what womans sonne,
Will sourely leaue her till he haue preuailed.
Aye me,but yet thou mighst my seate forbeare,
And chide thy beauty,and thy straying youth,
Who lead thee in their ryot euen there
Where thou art forst to breake a two fold truth:
　　Hers by thy beauty tempting her to thee,
　　Thine by thy beautie beeing false to me.

42

THat thou hast her it is not all my griefe,
　　And yet it may be said I lou'd her deerely,
That she hath thee is of my wayling cheefe,
A losse in loue that touches me more neerely.
Louing offendors thus I will excuse yee,
Thou doost loue her,because thou know'st I loue her,
And for my sake euen so doth she abuse me,
Suffring my friend for my sake to approoue her,
If I loose thee,my losse is my loues gaine,
And loosing her,my friend hath found that losse,
Both finde each other,and I loose both twaine,
And both for my sake lay on me this crosse,
　　But here's the ioy,my friend and I are one,
　　Sweete flattery,then she loues but me alone.

43

WHen most I winke then doe mine eyes best see,
　　For all the day they view things vnrespected,
But when I sleepe,in dreames they looke on thee,
And darkely bright,are bright in darke directed.
Then thou whose shaddow shaddowes doth make bright,
How would thy shadowes forme,forme happy show,
To the cleere day with thy much cleerer light,
When to vn-seeing eyes thy shade shines so?

How

How would (I say)mine eyes be blessed made,
By looking on thee in the liuing day?
When in dead night their faire imperfect shade,
Through heauy sleepe on sightlesse eyes doth stay?
  All dayes are nights to see till I see thee,
  And nights bright daies when dreams do shew thee me.

44

IF the dull substance of my flesh were thought,
Iniurious distance should not stop my way,
For then dispight of space I would be brought,
From limits farre remote,where thou doost stay,
No matter then although my foote did stand
Vpon the farthest earth remoou'd from thee,
For nimble thought can iumpe both sea and land,
As soone as thinke the place where he would be.
But ah,thought kil's me that I am not thought
To leape large lengths of miles when thou art gone,
But that so much of earth and water wrought,
I must attend,times leasure with my mone.
  Receiuing naughts by elements so sloe,
  But heauie teares,badges of eithers woe.

45

THe other two,slight ayre,and purging fire,
Are both with thee,where euer I abide,
The first my thought,the other my desire,
These present absent with swift motion slide.
For when these quicker Elements are gone
In tender Embassie of loue to thee,
My life being made of foure,with two alone,
Sinkes downe to death,opprest with melancholie.
Vntill liues compositiō be recured,
By those swift messengers return'd from thee,
Who euen but now come back againe assured,
Of their faire health,recounting it to me.
  This told,I ioy,but then no longer glad,
  I send them back againe and straight grow sad.

D 2

Mine

46

Mine eye and heart are at a mortall warre,
How to deuide the conqueſt of thy ſight,
Mine eye,my heart their pictures ſight would barre,
My heart,mine eye the freeedome of that right,
My heart doth plead that thou in him dooſt lye,
(A cloſet neuer pearſt with chriſtall eyes)
But the defendant doth that plea deny,
And ſayes in him their faire appearance lyes,
To ſide this title is impannelled
A queſt of thoughts,all tennants to the heart,
And by their verdict is determined
The cleere eyes moyitie,and the deare hearts part.
  As thus,mine eyes due is their outward part,
  And my hearts right,their inward loue of heart.

47

Betwixt mine eye and heart a league is tooke,
And each doth good turnes now vnto the other,
When that mine eye is famiſht for a looke,
Or heart in loue with ſighes himſelfe doth ſmother;
With my loues picture then my eye doth feaſt,
And to the painted banquet bids my heart:
An other time mine eye is my hearts gueſt,
And in his thoughts of loue doth ſhare a part,
So either by thy picture or my loue,
Thy ſeife away,are preſent ſtill with me,
For thou not farther then my thoughts canſt moue,
And I am ſtill with them,and they with thee.
  Or if they ſleepe,thy picture in my ſight
  Awakes my heart,to hearts and eyes delight.

48

How carefull was I when I tooke my way,
Each trifle vnder trueſt barres to thruſt,
That to my vſe it might vn-vſed ſtay
From hands of falſehood,in ſure wards of truſt?
But thou,to whom my iewels trifles are,

Most worthy comfort,now my greatest griefe,
Thou best of deerest,and mine onely care,
Art left the prey of euery vulgar theefe.
Thee haue I not lockt vp in any chest,
Saue where thou art not though I feele thou art,
Within the gentle closure of my brest,
From whence at pleasure thou maist come and part,
 And euen thence thou wilt be stolne I feare,
 For truth prooues theeuish for a prize so deare.

49

AGainst that time (if euer that time come)
When I shall see thee frowne on my defects,
When as thy loue hath cast his vtmost summe,
Cauld to that audite by aduis'd respects,
Against that time when thou shalt strangely passe,
And scarcely greete me with that sunne thine eye,
When loue conuerted from the thing it was
Shall reasons finde of setled grauitie.
Against that time do I insconce me here
Within the knowledge of mine owne desart,
And this my hand,against my selfe vpreare,
To guard the lawfull reasons on thy part,
 To leaue poore me,thou hast the strength of lawes,
 Since why to loue,I can alledge no cause.

50

HOw heauie doe I iourney on the way,
When what I seeke (my wearie trauels end)
Doth teach that ease and that repose to say
Thus farre the miles are measurde from thy friend.
The beast that beares me,tired with my woe,
Plods duly on,to beare that waight in me,
As if by some instinct the wretch did know
His rider lou'd not speed being made from thee:
The bloody spurre cannot prouoke him on,
That some-times anger thrusts into his hide,
Which heauily he answers with a grone,

More

More sharpe to me then spurring to his side,
  For that same grone doth put this in my mind,
  My greefe lies onward and my ioy behind.

51

THus can my loue excuse the flow offence,
  Of my dull bearer,when from thee I speed,
From where thou art,why shoulld I haft me thence,
Till I returne of posting is noe need.
O what excuse will my poore beast then find,
When swift extremity can seeme but slow,
Then should I spurre though mounted on the wind,
In winged speed no motion shall I know,
Then can no horse with my desire keepe pace,
Therefore desire(of perfects loue being made)
Shall naigh noe dull flesh in his fiery race,
But loue,for loue,thus shall excuse my iade,
  Since from thee going he went wilfull slow,
  Towards thee ile run,and giue him leaue to goe.

52

SO am I as the rich whose blessed key,
  Can bring him to his sweet vp-locked treasure,
The which he will not eu'ry hower suruay,
For blunting the fine point of seldome pleasure.
Therefore are feasts so sollemne and so rare,
Since sildom comming in the long yeare set,
Like stones of worth they thinly placed are,
Or captaine Iewells in the carconet.
So is the time that keepes you as my chest,
Or as the ward-robe which the robe doth hide,
To make some speciall instant speciall blest,
By new vnfoulding his imprison'd pride.
  Blessed are you whose worthinesse giues skope,
  Being had to tryumph,being lackt to hope.

53

WHat is your substance,whereof are you made,
  That millions of strange shaddowes on you tend?
                        Since

Since euery one,hath euery one,one shade,
And you but one,can euery shaddow lend:
Describe *Adonis* and the counterfet,
Is poorely immitated after you,
On *Hellens* cheeke all art of beautie set,
And you in *Grecian* tires are painted new:
Speake of the spring,and foyzon of the yeare,
The one doth shaddow of your beautie show,
The other as your bountie doth appeare,
And you in euery blessed shape we know.
  In all externall grace you haue some part,
  But you like none,none you for constant heart.

54

OH how much more doth beautie beautious seeme,
  By that sweet ornament which truth doth giue,
The Rose lookes faire, but fairer we it deeme
For that sweet odor,which doth in it liue:
The Canker-bloomes haue full as deepe a die,
As the perfumed tincture of the Roses,
Hang on such thornes,and play as wantonly,
When sommers breath their masked buds discloses:
But for their virtue only is their show,
They liue vnwoo'd, and vnrespected fade,
Die to themselues . Sweet Roses doe not so,
Of their sweet deathes, are sweetest odors made:
  And so of you,beautious and louely youth,
  When that shall vade,by verse distils your truth.

55

NOt marble, nor the guilded monument,
  Of Princes shall out-liue this powrefull rime,
But you shall shine more bright in these contents
Then vnswept stone, besmeer'd with sluttish time.
When wastefull warre shall *Statues* ouer-turne,
And broiles roote out the worke of masonry,
Nor *Mars* his sword, nor warres quick fire shall burne:
The liuing record of your memory.

Gainst

Gainft death,and all obliuious emnity
Shall you pace forth, your praife fha'l ftil finde roome,
Euen in the eyes of all pofterity
That weare this world out to the ending doome.
  So til the iudgement that your felfe arife,
  You liue in this,and dwell in louers eies.

56

S weet loue renew thy force , be it not faid
  Thy edge fhould blunter be then apetite,
Which but too daie by feeding is alaied,
To morrow fharpned in his former might,
So loue be thou,although too daie thou fill
Thy hungrie eies,euen till they winck with fulneffe,
Too morrow fee againe,and doe not kill
The fpirit of Loue,with a perpetual dulneffe:
Let this fad *Intrim* like the Ocean be
Which parts the fhore,where two contracted new,
Come daily to the banckes,that when they fee:
Returne of loue,more bleff may be the view.
  As cal it Winter,which being ful of care,
  Makes Sômers welcome,thrice more wifh'd,more rare :

57

B Eing your flaue what fhould I doe but tend,
  Vpon the houres,and times of your defire?
I haue no precious time at al to fpend;
Nor feruices to doe til you require.
Nor dare I chide the world without end houre,
Whilft I(my foueraine)watch the clock for you,
Nor thinke the bitterneffe of abfence fowre,
VVhen you haue bid your feruant once adieue,
Nor dare I queftion with my iealious thought,
VVhere you may be,or your affaires fuppofe,
But like a fad flaue ftay and thinke of nought
Saue where you are , how happy you make thofe.
  So true a foole is loue,that in your Will,
  (Though you doe any thing)he thinkes no ill.

58

THat God forbid,that made me firſt your ſlaue,
I ſhould in thought controule your times of pleaſure,
Or at your hand th' **account** of houres to craue,
Being your vaſſail bound to ſtaie your leiſure.
Oh let me ſuffer(being at your beck)
Th' impriſon'd abſence of your libertie,
And patience tame,to ſufferance bide **each check**,
Without accuſing you of iniury.
Be where you liſt,your charter is ſo ſtrong,
That you your ſelfe may priuiledge your time
To what you will,to you it doth belong,
Your ſelfe to pardon of ſelfe-doing crime.
    I am to waite,though waiting ſo be hell,
    Not blame your pleaſure be it ill or well.

59

IF their bee nothing new,but that which is,
Hath beene before , how are our braines beguild,
Which laboring for inuention beare amiſſe
The ſecond burthen of a former child ?
Oh that record could with a back-ward looke,
Euen of fiue hundreth courſes of the Sunne,
Show me your image in ſome antique booke,
Since minde at firſt in carrecter was done.
That I might ſee what the old world could ſay,
To this compoſed wonder of your frame,
Whether we are mended,or where better they,
Or whether reuolution be the ſame.
    Oh ſure I am the wits of former daies,
    To ſubiects worſe haue giuen admiring praiſe.

60

LIke as the waues make towards the pibled ſhore,
So do our minuites haſten to their end,
Each changing place with that which goes before,
In ſequent toile all forwards do contend.
Natiuity once in the maine of light,

E   Crawls

Crawles to maturity, wherewith being crown'd,
Crooked eclipses gainst his glory fight,
And time that gaue, doth now his gift confound.
Time doth transfixe the florish set on youth,
And delues the paralels in beauties brow,
Feedes on the rarities of natures truth,
And nothing stands but for his sieth to mow.
   And yet to times in hope, my verse shall stand
   Praising thy worth, dispight his cruell hand.

61

IS it thy wil, thy Image should keepe open
My heauy eie ids to the weary night?
Dost thou desire my slumbers should be broken,
While shadowes like to thee do mocke my sight?
Is it thy spirit that thou send'st from thee
So farre from home into my deeds to prye,
To find out shames and idle houres in me,
The skope and tenure of thy Ieloufie?
O no, thy loue though much, is not so great,
It is my loue that keepes mine eie awake,
Mine owne true loue that doth my rest defeat,
To plaie the watch-man euer for thy sake.
   For thee watch I, whilst thou dost wake elsewhere,
   From me farre of, with others all to neere.

63

SInne of selfe-loue possesseth al mine eie,
And all my soule, and al my euery part;
And for this sinne there is no remedie,
It is so grounded inward in my heart.
Me thinkes no face so gratious is as mine,
No shape so true, no truth of such account,
And for my selfe mine owne worth do define,
As I all other in all worths surmount.
But when my glasse shewes me my selfe indeed
Beated and chopt with tand antiquitie,
Mine owne selfe loue quite contrary I read

Selfe

Selfe, so selfe louing were iniquity,
   T'is thee(my selfe)that for my selfe I praise,
   Painting my age with beauty of thy daies,

63

AGainst my loue shall be as I am now
   With times iniurious hand chrusht and ore-worne,
When houres haue dreind his blood and fild his brow
With lines and wrincles, when his youthfull morne
Hath trauaild on to Ages steepie night,
And all those beauties whereof now he's King
Are vanishing, or vanisht out of sight,
Stealing away the treasure of his Spring.
For such a time do I now fortifie
Against confounding Ages cruell knife,
That he shall neuer cut from memory
My sweet loues beauty, though my louers life.
   His beautie shall in these blacke lines be seene,
   And they shall liue, and he in them still greene.

64

VVHen I haue seene by times fell hand defaced
   The rich proud cost of outworne buried age,
When sometime loftie towers I see downe rased,
And brasse eternall slaue to mortall rage.
When I haue seene the hungry Ocean gaine
Aduantage on the Kingdome of the shoare,
And the firme soile win of the watry maine,
Increasing store with losse, and losse with store.
When I haue seene such interchange of state,
Or state it selfe confounded, to decay,
Ruine hath taught me thus to ruminate
That Time will come and take my loue away.
   This thought is as a death which cannot choose
   But weepe to haue, that which it feares to loose.

65

SInce brasse, nor stone, nor earth, nor boundlesse sea,
   But sad mortallity ore-swaies their power,

E2   How

How with this rage shall beautie hold a plea,
Whose action is no stronger then a flower?
O how shall summers huimy breath hold out,
Against the wrackfull siedge of battring dayes,
When rocks impregnable are not so stoute,
Nor gates of steele so strong but time decayes?
O fearefull meditation, where alack,
Shall times best Iewell from times chest lie hid?
Or what strong hand can hold his swift foote back,
Or who his spoile or beautie can forbid?
　　O none, vnlesse this miracle haue might,
　　That in black inck my loue may still shine bright.

66

TYr'd with all these for restfull death I cry,
　As to behold desert a begger borne,
And needie Nothing trimd in iollitie,
And purest faith vnhappily forsworne,
And gilded honor shamefully misplast,
And maiden vertue rudely strumpeted,
And right perfection wrongfully disgrac'd,
And strength by limping sway disabled,
And arte made tung-tide by authoritie,
And Folly (Doctor-like) controuling skill,
And simple-Truth miscalde Simplicitie,
And captiue-good attending Captaine ill.
　　Tyr'd with all these, from these would I be gone,
　　Saue that to dye, I leaue my loue alone.

67

AH wherefore with infection should he liue,
　And with his presence grace impietie,
That sinne by him aduantage should atchiue,
And lace it selfe with his societie?
Why should false painting immitate his cheeke,
And steale dead seeing of his liuing hew?
Why should poore beautie indirectly seeke,
Roses of shaddow, since his Rose is true?

Why

Why fhould he liue,now nature banckrout is,
Beggerd of blood to blufh through liuely vaines,
For fhe hath no exchecker now but his,
And proud of many,liues vpon his gaines?
    O him fhe ftores,to fhow what welth fhe had,
    In daies long fince,before thefe laft fo bad.

68

THis is his cheeke the map of daies out-worne,
    When beauty liu'd and dy'ed as flowers do now,
Before thefe baftard fignes of faire were borne,
Or durft inhabit on a liuing brow:
Before the goulden treffes of the dead,
The right of fepulchers,were fhorne away,
To liue a fcond life on fecond head,
Ere beauties dead fleece made another gay:
In him thofe holy antique howers are feene,
Without all ornament,it felfe and true,
Making no fummer of an others greene,
Robbing no ould to dreffe his beauty new,
    And him as for a map doth Nature ftore,
    To fhew faulfe Art what beauty was of yore.

69

THofe parts of thee that the worlds eye doth view,
    Want nothing that the thought of hearts can mend:
All toungs(the voice of foules)giue thee that end,
Vttring bare truth,euen fo as foes Commend.
Their outward thus with outward praife is crownd,
But thofe fame toungs that giue thee fo thine owne,
In other accents doe this praife confound
By feeing farther then the eye hath fhowne.
They looke into the beauty of thy mind,
And that in gueffe they meafure by thy deeds,
Then churls their thoughts(although their eies were kind)
To thy faire flower ad the rancke fmell of weeds,
    But why thy odor matcheth not thy fhow,
    The folye is this,that thou doeft common grow.

Thai

70

THat thou are blam'd shall not be thy defect,
  For slanders marke was euer yet the faire,
The ornament of beauty is suspect,
A Crow that flies in heauens sweetest ayre.
So thou be good,slander doth but approue,
Their worth the greater beeing woo'd of time,
For Canker vice the sweetest buds doth loue,
And thou present'st a pure vntayined prime.
Thou hast past by the ambush of young daies,
Either not assayld,or victor beeing charg'd,
Yet this thy praise cannot be soe thy praise,
To tye vp enuy,euermore inlarged,
    If some suspect of ill maskt not thy show,
    Then thou alone kingdomes of hearts shouldst owe.

71

NOe Longer mourne for me when I am dead,
  Then you shall heare the surly sullen bell
Giue warning to the world that I am fled
From this vile world with vildest wormes to dwell:
Nay if you read this line,remember not,
The hand that writ it,for I loue you so,
That I in your sweet thoughts would be forgot,
If thinking on me then should make you woe.
O if(I say)you looke vpon this verse,
When I (perhaps) compounded am with clay,
Do not so much as my poore name reherse;
But let your loue euen with my life decay.
    Least the wise world should looke into your mone,
    And mocke you with me after I am gon.

72

O Least the world should taske you to recite,
    What merit liu'd in me that you should loue
After my death(deare loue)for get me quite,
For you in me can nothing worthy proue.
Vnlesse you would deuise some vertuous lye,

To doe more for me then mine owne defert,
And hang more praife vpon deceafed I,
Then nigard truth would willingly impart:
O leaft your true loue may feeme falce in this,
That you for loue fpeake well of me vntrue,
My name be buried where my body is,
And liue no more to fhame nor me, nor you.
 For I am fham'd by that which I bring forth,
 And fo fhould you, to loue things nothing worth.

73

THat time of yeeare thou maift in me behold,
 When yellow leaues, or none, or few doe hange
Vpon thofe boughes which fhake againft the could,
Bare rn'wd quiers, where late the fweet birds fang.
In me thou feeft the twi-light of fuch day,
As after Sun-fet fadeth in the Weft,
Which by and by blacke night doth take away,
Deaths fecond felfe that feals vp all in reft.
In me thou feeft the glowing of fuch fire,
That on the afhes of his youth doth lye,
As the death bed, whereon it muft expire,
Confum'd with that which it was nurrifht by.
 This thou perceu'ft, which makes thy loue more ftrong,
 To loue that well, which thou muft leaue ere long.

74

BVt be contented when that fell areft,
 With out all bayle fhall carry me away,
My life hath in this line fome intereft,
Which for memoriall ftill with thee fhall ftay.
When thou reueweft this, thou doeft reuew,
The very part was confecrate to thee,
The earth can haue but earth, which is his due,
My fpirit is thine the better part of me,
So then thou haft but loft the dregs of life,
The pray of wormes, my body being dead,
The coward conqueft of a wretches knife,

To

To bafe of thee to be remembred,
   The worth of that, is that which it containes,
   And that is this, and this with thee remaines.

75

SO are you to my thoughts as food to life,
   Or as fweet feaſon'd ſhewers are to the ground;
And for the peace of you I hold ſuch ſtrife,
As twixt a miſer and his wealth is found.
Now proud as an inioyer, and anon
Doubting the filching age will ſteale his treaſure,
Now counting beſt to be with you alone,
Then betterd that the world may fee my pleaſure,
Some-time all ful with feaſting on your ſight,
And by and by cleane ſtarued for a looke,
Poſſeſſing or purſuing no delight
Saue what is had, or muſt from you be tooke.
   Thus do I pine and ſurfet day by day,
   Or gluttoning on all, or all away,

76

VVHy is my verſe fo barren of new pride?
   So far from variation or quicke change?
Why with the time do I not glance aſide
To new found methods, and to compounds ſtrange?
Why write I ſtill all one, euer the fame,
And keepe inuention in a noted weed,
That euery word doth almoſt fel my name,
Shewing their birth, and where they did proceed?
O know fweet loue I alwaies write of you,
And you and loue are ſtill my argument:
So all my beſt is dreſſing old words new,
Spending againe what is already ſpent:
   For as the Sun is daily new and old,
   So is my loue ſtill telling what is told,

77

THy glaſſe will ſhew thee how thy beauties were,
   Thy dyall how thy precious mynuits waſte,

The

The vacant leaues thy mindes imprint will beare,
And of this booke,this learning maist thou taste,
The wrinckles which thy glasse will truly show,
Of mouthed graues will giue thee memorie,
Thou by thy dyals shady stealth maist know,
Times theeuish progresse to eternitie.
Looke what thy memorie cannot containe,
Commit to these waste blacks,and thou shalt finde
Those children nurst,deliuerd from thy braine,
To take a new acquaintance of thy minde.
   These offices,so oft as thou wilt looke,
   Shall profit thee,and much inrich thy booke.

78

SO oft haue I inuok'd thee for my Muse,
  And found such faire assistance in my verse,
As euery *Alien* pen hath got my vse,
And vnder thee their poesie disperse.
Thine eyes, that taught the dumbe on high to sing,
And heauie ignorance aloft to flee,
Haue added fethers to the learneds wing,
And giuen grace a double Maiestie.
Yet be most proud of that which I compile,
Whose influence is thine,and borne of thee.
In others workes thou doost but mend the stile,
And Arts with thy sweete graces graced be.
   But thou art all my art,and doost aduance
   As high as learning,my rude ignorance.

79

WHilst I alone did call vpon thy ayde,
  My verse alone had all thy gentle grace,
But now my gracious numbers are decayde,
And my sick Muse doth giue an other place.
I grant (sweet loue)thy louely argument
Deserues the trauaile of a worthier pen,
Yet what of thee thy Poet doth inuent,
He robs thee of,and payes it thee againe,

F

He

He lends thee vertue, and he ſtole that word,
From thy behauiour, beautie doth he giue
And found it in thy cheeke: he can affoord
No praiſe to thee, but what in thee doth liue.
 Then thanke him not for that which he doth ſay,
 Since what he owes thee, thou thy ſelfe dooſt pay,

80

O How I faint when I of you do write,
 Knowing a better ſpirit doth vſe your name,
And in the praiſe thereof ſpends all his might,
To make me toung-tide ſpeaking of your fame.
But ſince your worth (wide as the Ocean is)
The humble as the proudeſt ſaile doth beare,
My ſawſie barke (inferior farre to his)
On your broad maine doth wilfully appeare.
Your ſhalloweſt helpe will hold me vp a floate,
Whilſt he vpon your ſoundleſſe deepe doth ride,
Or (being wrackt) I am a worthleſſe bote,
He of tall building, and of goodly pride.
 Then If he thriue and I be caſt away,
 The worſt was this, my loue was my decay.

81

OR I ſhall liue your Epitaph to make,
 Or you ſuruiue when I in earth am rotten,
From hence your memory death cannot take,
Although in me each part will be forgotten.
Your name from hence immortall life ſhall haue,
Though I (once gone) to all the world muſt dye,
The earth can yeeld me but a common graue,
When you intombed in mens eyes ſhall lye,
Your monument ſhall be my gentle verſe,
Which eyes not yet created ſhall ore-read,
And toungs to be, your beeing ſhall rehearſe,
When all the breathers of this world are dead,
 You ſtill ſhall liue (ſuch vertue hath my Pen)
 Where breath moſt breaths, euen in the mouths of men.

I grant

82

I Grant thou wert not married to my Muse,
And therefore maiest without attaint ore-looke
The dedicated words which writers vse
Of their faire subiect,blessing euery booke.
Thou art as faire in knowledge as in hew,
Finding thy worth a limmit past my praise,
And therefore art inforc'd to seeke anew,
Some fresher stampe of the time bettering dayes.
And do so loue,yet when they haue deuisde,
What strained touches Rhethorick can lend,
Thou truly faire,wert truly simpathizde,
In true plaine words,by thy true telling friend.
   And their grosse painting might be better vs'd,
   Where cheekes need blood,in thee it is abus'd.

83

I Neuer saw that you did painting need,
And therefore to your faire no painting set,
I found (or thought I found) you did exceed,
The barren tender of a Poets debt :
And therefore haue I slept in your report,
That you your selfe being extant well might show,
How farre a moderne quill doth come to short,
Speaking of worth,what worth in you doth grow,
This silence for my sinne you did impute,
Which shall be most my glory being dombe,
For I impaire not beautie being mute,
When others would giue life,and bring a tombe.
   There liues more life in one of your faire eyes,
   Then both your Poets can in praise deuise.

84

WHo is it that sayes most,which can say more,
Then this rich praise,that you alone,are you,
In whose confine immured is the store,
Which should example where your equall grew,
Leane penurie within that Pen doth dwell,

                 That

That to his subiect lends not some small glory,
But he that writes of you,if he can tell,
That you are you,so dignifies his story.
Let him but coppy what in you is writ,
Not making worse what nature made so cleere,
And such a counter-part shall fame his wit,
Making his stile admired euery where.
   You to your beautious blessings adde a curse,
    Being fond'on praise,which makes your praises worse.

85

MY toung-tide Muse in manners holds her still,
While comments of your praise richly compil'd,
Reserue their Character with goulden quill,
And precious phrase by all the Muses fil'd.
I thinke good thoughts,whilst other write good wordes,
And like vnlettered clarke still crie Amen,
To euery Himne that able spirit affords,
In polisht for ne of well refined pen.
Hearing you praisd,I say 'tis so, 'tis true,
And to the most of praise adde some-thing more,
But that is in my thought,whose loue to you
(Though words come hind-most)holds his ranke before,
   Then others,for the breath of words respect,
    Me for my dombe thoughts,speaking in effect.

86

VVAs it the proud full saile of his great verse,
Bound for the prize of (all to precious) you,
That did my ripe thoughts in my braine inhearce,
Making their tombe the wombe wherein they grew?
Was it his spirit,by spirits taught to write.
Aboue a mortall pitch,that struck me dead?
No,neither he,nor his compiers by night
Giuing him ayde,my verse astonished.
He nor that affable familiar ghost
Which nightly gulls him with intelligence,
As victors of my silence cannot boast,

                        I was

I was not sick of any feare from thence.
　　But when your countinance fild vp his line,
　　Then lackt I matter, that infeebled mine.

87

FArewell thou art too deare for my poſſeſſing,
And like enough thou knowſt thy eſtimate,
The Cha ter of thy worth giues thee releaſing:
My bonds in thee are all determinate.
For how do I hold thee but by thy granting,
And for that ritches where is my deſeruing?
The cauſe of this faire guiſt in me is wanting,
And ſo my pattent back againe is ſweruing.
Thy ſelfe thou gau'ſt, thy owne worth then not knowing,
Or mee to whom thou gau'ſt it, elſe miſtaking,
So thy great guiſt vpon miſpriſion growing,
Comes home againe, on better iudgement making.
　　Thus haue I had thee as a dreame doth flatter,
　　In ſleepe a King, but waking no ſuch matter.

88

VVHen thou ſhalt be diſpode to ſet me light,
　　And place my merrit in the eie of ſkorne,
Vpon thy ſide, againſt my ſelfe ile fight,
And proue thee virtuous, though thou art forſworne:
With mine owne weakeneſſe being beſt acquainted,
Vpon thy part I can ſet downe a ſtory
Of faults conceald, wherein I am attainted :
That thou in looſing me ſhall win much glory:
And I by this wil be a gainer too,
For bending all my louing thoughts on thee,
The iniuries that to my ſelfe I doe,
Doing thee vantage, duble vantage me.
　　Such is my loue, to thee I ſo belong,
　　That for thy right, my ſelfe will beare all wrong.

89

SAy that thou didſt forſake mee for ſome falt,
And I will comment vpon that offence,

　　　　　　　　　The

Speake of my lamenesse, and I straight will halt:
Against thy reasons making no defence.
Thou canst not(loue)disgrace me halfe so ill,
To set a forme vpon desired change,
As ile my selfe disgrace,knowing thy wil,
I will acquaintance strangle and looke strange:
Be absent from thy walkes and in my tongue,
Thy sweet beloued name no more shall dwell,
Least I(too much prophane)should do it wronge:
And haplie of our old acquaintance tell.
    For thee,against my selfe ile vow debate,
    For I must nere loue him whom thou dost hate.

90

THen hate me when thou wilt, if euer,now,
    Now while the world is bent my deeds to crosse.
Ioyne with the spight of fortune,make me bow,
And doe not drop in for an after losse:
Ah doe not,when my heart hath scapte this sorrow,
Come in the rereward of a conquerd woe,
Giue not a windy night a rainie morrow,
To linger out a purposd ouer-throw.
If thou wilt leaue me, do not leaue me last,
When other pettie griefes haue done their spight,
But in the onset come,so shall I taste
At first the very worst of fortunes might.
    And other straines of woe, which now seeme woe,
    Compar'd with losse of thee,will not seeme so.

91

SOme glory in their birth,some in their skill,
    Some in their wealth, some in their bodies force,
Some in their garments though new-fangled ill:
Some in their Hawkes and Hounds,some in their Horse,
And euery humor hath his adiunct pleasure,
Wherein it findes a ioy aboue the rest,
But these perticulers are not my measure,
All these I better in one generall best.

                                        Thy

Thy loue is bitter then high birth to me,
Richer then wealth, prouder then garments coft,
Of more delight then Hawkes or Horfes bee:
And hauing thee, of all mens pride I boaft,
    Wretched in this alone, that thou maift take,
    All this away, and me moft wretched make.

92

BVt doe thy worft to fteale thy felfe away,
For tearme of life thou art affured mine,
And life no longer then thy loue will ftay,
For it depends vpon that loue of thine.
Then need I not to feare the worft of wrongs,
When in the leaft of them my life hath end,
I fee, a better ftate to me belongs
Then that, which on thy humor doth depend.
Thou canft not vex me with inconftant minde,
Since that my life on thy reuolt doth lie,
Oh what a happy title do I finde,
Happy to haue thy loue, happy to die!
    But whats fo bleffed faire that feares no blot,
    Thou maift be falce, and yet I know it not.

93

SO fhall I liue, fuppofing thou art true,
Like a deceiued husband fo loues face,
May ftill feeme loue to me, though alter'd new:
Thy lookes with me, thy heart in other place.
For their can liue no hatred in thine eye,
Therefore in that I cannot know thy change,
In manies lookes, the falce hearts hiftory
Is writ in moods and frounes and wrinckles ftrange.
But heauen in thy creation did decree,
That in thy face fweet loue fhould euer dwell,
What ere thy thoughts, or thy hearts workings be,
Thy lookes fhould nothing thence, but fweetneffe tell.
    How like *Eaues* apple doth thy beauty grow,
    If thy fweet vertue anfwere not thy fhow.

94

They that haue powre to hurt,and will doe none,
That doe not do the thing,they moſt do ſhowe,
Who mouing others,are themſelues as ſtone,
Vnmooued,could,and to temptation ſlow:
They rightly do inherrit heauens graces,
And husband natures ritches from expence,
They are the Lords and owners of their faces,
Others,but ſtewards of their excellence:
The ſommers flowre is to the ſommer ſweet,
Though to it ſelfe,it onely liue and die,
But if that flowre with baſe infection meete,
The baſeſt weed out-braues his dignity:
   For ſweeteſt things turne ſowreſt by their deedes,
   Lillies that feſter,ſmell far worſe then weeds.

95

How ſweet and louely doſt thou make the ſhame,
Which like a canker in the fragrant Roſe,
Doth ſpot the beautie of thy budding name?
Oh in what ſweets doeſt thou thy ſinnes incloſe!
That tongue that tells the ſtory of thy daies,
(Making laſciuious comments on thy ſport)
Cannot diſpraiſe,but in a kinde of praiſe,
Naming thy name,bleſſes an ill report.
Oh what a manſion haue thoſe vices got,
Which for their habitation choſe out thee,
Where beauties vaile doth couer euery blot,
And all things turnes to faire,that eies can ſee!
   Take heed(deare heart)of this large priuiledge,
   The hardeſt knife ill vſ'd doth looſe his edge.

96

Some ſay thy fault is youth,ſome wantoneſſe,
Some ſay thy grace is youth and gentle ſport,
Both grace and faults are lou'd of more and leſſe:
Thou makſt faults graces,that to thee reſort:
As on the finger of a throned Queene,

The

The basest Iewell wil be well esteem'd:
So are those errors that in thee are seene,
To truths tranflated, and for true things deem'd.
How many Lambs might the sterne Wolfe betray,
If like a Lambe he could his lookes tranflate,
How many gazers mighst thou lead away,
If thou wouldst vfe the strength of all thy state?
   But doe not so, I loue thee in fuch fort,
    As thou being mine, mine is thy good report.

97

How like a Winter hath my abfence beene
From thee, the pleafure of the fleeting yeare?
   What freezings haue I felt, what darke daies feene?
What old Decembers barenesse euery where?
And yet this time remou'd was fommers time,
The teeming Autumne big with ritch increase,
Bearing the wanton burthen of the prime,
Like widdowed wombes after their Lords deceafe:
Yet this aboundant issue seem'd to me,
But hope of Orphans, and vn-fathered fruite,
For Sommer and his pleafures waite on thee,
And thou away, the very birds are mute.
   Or if they fing, tis with fo dull a cheere,
    That leaues looke pale, dreading the Winters neere.

98

From you haue I beene abfent in the fpring,
When proud pide Aprill (dreft in all his trim)
Hath put a fpirit of youth in euery thing:
That heauie *Saturne* laught and leapt with him.
Yet nor the laies of birds, nor the fweet fmell
Of different flowers in odor and in hew,
Could make me any fummers story tell:
Or from their proud lap pluck them where they grew:
Nor did I wonder at the Lillies white,
Nor praife the deepe vermillion in the Rofe,
They weare but fweet, but figures of delight:

G   Drawne

Drawne after you, you patterne of all those.
  Yet seem'd it Winter still,and you away,
  As with your shaddow I with these did play.

99

THe forward violet thus did I chide,
  Sweet theefe whence didst thou steale thy sweet that
If not from my loues breath,the purple pride,   (smels
Which on thy soft cheeke for complexion dwells?
In my loues veines thou hast too grosely died,
The Lillie I condemned for thy hand,
And buds of marierom had stolne thy haire,
The Roses fearefully on thornes did stand,
Our blushing shame,an other white dispaire:
A third nor red,nor white,had stolne of both,
And to his robbry had annext thy breath,
But for his theft in pride of all his growth
A vengfull canker eate him vp to death.
  More flowers I noted,yet I none could see,
  But sweet,or culler it had stolne from thee.

100

VVHere art thou Muse that thou forgetst so long,
  To speake of that which giues thee all thy might?
Spendst thou thy furie on some worthlesse songe,
Darkning thy powre to lend base subiects light.
Returne forgetfull Muse,and straight redeeme,
In gentle numbers time so idely spent,
Sing to the eare that doth thy laies esteeme,
And giues thy pen both skill and argument.
Rise resty Muse,my loues sweet face suruay,
If time haue any wrincle grauen there,
If any,be a Satire to decay,
And make times spoiles dispised euery where.
  Giue my loue fame faster then time wasts life,
  So thou preuenst his sieth,and crooked knife.

101

OH truant Muse what shalbe thy amends,

For thy neglect of truth in beauty di'd?
Both truth and beauty on my loue depends:
So dost thou too,and therein dignifi'd:
Make answere Muse,wilt thou not haply saie,
Truth needs no collour with his collour fixt,
Beautie no pensell,beauties truth to lay:
But best is best,if neuer intermixt.
Because he needs no praise,wilt thou be dumb?
Excuse not silence so,for't lies in thee,
To make him much out-liue a gilded tombe:
And to be prais'd of ages yet to be.
    Then do thy office Muse,I teach thee how,
    To make him seeme long hence,as he showes now.

102

MY loue is strengthned though more weake in see-
I loue not lesse,thogh lesse the show appeare, (ming
That loue is marchandiz'd,whose ritch esteeming,
The owners tongue doth publish euery where.
Our loue was new,and then but in the spring,
When I was wont to greet it with my laies,
As *Philomell* in summers front doth singe,
And stops his pipe in growth of riper daies:
Not that the summer is lesse pleasant now
Then when her mournefull himns did hush the night,
But that wild musick burthens euery bow,
And sweets growne common loose their deare delight.
    Therefore like her,I some-time hold my tongue:
    Because I would not dull you with my songe.

103

ALack what pouerty my Muse brings forth,
That hauing such a skope to show her pride,
The argument all bare is of more worth
Then when it hath my added praise beside.
Oh blame me not if I no more can write!
Looke in your glasse and there appeares a face,
That ouer-goes my blunt inuention quite,
Dulling my lines,and doing me disgrace.

         Were

Were it not sinfull then striuing to mend,
To marre the subiect that before was well,
For to no other passe my verses tend,
Then of your graces and your gifts to tell.
    And more,much more then in my verse can sit,
    Your owne glasse showes you,when you looke in it.

104

TO me faire friend you neuer can be old,
  For as you were when first your eye I eyde,
Such seemes your beautie still:Three Winters colde,
Haue from the forrests shooke three summers pride,
Three beautious springs to yellow _Autumne_ turn'd,
In processe of the seasons haue I seene,
Three Aprill perfumes in three hot Iunes burn'd,
Since first I saw you fresh which yet are greene.
Ah yet doth beauty like a Dyall hand,
Steale from his figure,and no pace perceiu'd,
So your sweete hew,which me thinkes still doth stand
Hath motion,and mine eye may be deceaued.
    For feare of which,heare this thou age vnbred,
    Ere you were borne was beauties summer dead,

105

LEt not my loue be cal'd Idolatrie,
  Nor my beloued as an Idoll show,
Since all alike my songs and praises be
To one,of one,still such,and euer so.
Kinde is my loue to day,to morrow kinde,
Still constant in a wondrous excellence,
Therefore my verse to constancie confin'de,
One thing expressing,leaues out difference.
Faire,kinde,and true,is all my argument,
Faire,kinde and true,varrying to other words,
And in this change is my inuention spent,
Three theams in one,which wondrous scope affords.
    Faire,kinde,and true,haue often liu'd alone.
    Which three till now,neuer kept seate in one.

When

106

WHen in the Chronicle of wasted time,
　　I see discriptions of the fairest wights,
And beautie making beautifull old rime,
In praise of Ladies dead, and louely Knights,
Then in the blazon of sweet beauties best,
Of hand, of foote, of lip, of eye, of brow,
I see their antique Pen would haue exprest,
Euen such a beauty as you maister now.
So all their praises are but prophesies
Of this our time, all you prefiguring,
And for they look'd but with deuining eyes,
They had not still enough your worth to sing :
　　For we which now behold these present dayes,
　　Haue eyes to wonder, but lack toungs to praise.

107

NOt mine owne feares, nor the prophetick soule,
　　Of the wide world, dreaming on things to come,
Can yet the lease of my true loue controule,
Supposde as forfeit to a confin'd doome.
The mortall Moone hath her eclipse indur'de,
And the sad Augurs mock their owne presage,
Incertenties now crowne them-selues assur'de,
And peace proclaimes Oliues of endlesse age.
Now with the drops of this most balmie time,
My loue lookes fresh, and death to me subscribes,
Since spight of him Ile liue in this poore rime,
While he insults ore dull and speachlesse tribes.
　　And thou in this shalt finde thy monument,
　　When tyrants crests and tombs of brasse are spent.

108

WHat's in the braine that Inck may character,
　　Which hath not figur'd to thee my true spirit,
What's new to speake, what now to register,
That may expresse my loue, or thy deare merit?
Nothing sweet boy, but yet like prayers diuine,

　　　　　　　　　　I must

I muſt each day ſay ore the very ſame,
Counting no old thing old,thou mine,I thine,
Euen as when firſt I hallowed thy faire name,
So that eternall loue in loues freſh caſe,
Waighes not the duſt and iniury of age,
Nor giues to neceſſary wrinckles place,
But makes antiquitie for aye his page,
   Finding the firſt conceit of loue there bred,
   Where time and outward forme would ſhew it dead,

109

ONeuer ſay that I was falſe of heart,
   Though abſence ſeem'd my flame to quallifie,
As eaſie might I from my ſelfe depart,
As from my ſoule which in thy breſt doth lye :
That is my home of loue,if I haue rang'd,
Like him that trauels I returne againe,
Iuſt to the time,not with the time exchang'd,
So that my ſelfe bring water for my ſtaine,
Neuer beleeue though in my nature raign'd,
All frailties that beſiege all kindes of blood,
That it could ſo prepoſterouſlie be ſtain'd,
To leaue for nothing all thy ſumme of good :
   For nothing this wide Vniuerſe I call,
   Saue thou my Roſe,in it thou art my all.

110

ALas,'tis true,I haue gone here and there,
   And made my ſelfe a motley to the view,
Gor'd mine own thoughts,ſold cheap what is moſt deare,
Made old offences of affections new.
Moſt true it is,that I haue lookt on truth
Aſconce and ſtrangely: But by all aboue,
Theſe blenches gaue my heart an other youth,
And worſe eſſaies prou'd thee my beſt of loue,
Now all is done,haue what ſhall haue no end,
Mine appetite I neuer more will grin'de
On newer proofe,to trie an older friend,
A God in loue,to whom I am confin'd.

Then

Then giue me welcome,next my heauen the best,
Euen to thy pure and most most louing brest.

111

O For my sake doe you wish fortune chide,
The guiltie goddesse of my harmfull deeds,
That did not better for my life prouide,
Then publick meanes which publick manners breeds.
Thence comes it that my name receiues a brand,
And almost thence my nature is subdu'd
To what it workes in,like the Dyers hand,
Pitty me then,and wish I were renu'de,
Whilst like a willing pacient I will drinke,
Potions of Eysell gainst my strong infection,
No bitternesse that I will bitter thinke,
Nor double pennance to correct correction.
   Pittie me then deare friend,and I assure yee,
   Euen that your pittie is enough to cure mee.

112

YOur loue and pittie doth th'impression fill,
Which vulgar scandall stampt vpon my brow,
For what care I who calles me well or ill,
So you ore-greene my bad,my good alow?
You are my All the world,and I must striue,
To know my shames and praises from your tounge,
None else to me,nor I to none aliue,
That my steel'd sence or changes right or wrong,
In so profound *Abisme* I throw all care
Of others voyces,that my Adders sence,
To cryttick and to flatterer stopped are:
Marke how with my neglect I doe dispence.
   You are so strongly in my purpose bred,
   That all the world besides me thinkes y'are dead.

113

SInce I left you,mine eye is in my minde,
And that which gouernes me to goe about,
Doth part his function,and is partly blind,

                           Seemes

Seemes feeing, but effectually is out:
For it no forme deliuers to the heart
Of bird, of flowre, or fhape which it doth lack,
Of his quick obiects hath the minde no part,
Nor his owne vifion houlds what it doth catch:
For if it fee the rud'ft or gentleft fight,
The moft fweet-fauor or deformedft creature,
The mountaine, or the fea, the day, or night:
The Croe, or Doue, it fhapes them to your feature.
    Incapable of more repleat, with you,
    My moft true minde thus maketh mine vntrue.

114

OR whether doth my minde being crown'd with you
Drinke vp the monarks plague this flattery?
Or whether fhall I fay mine eie faith true,
And that your loue taught it this *Alcumie*?
To make of monfters, and things indigeft,
Such cherubines as your fweet felfe refemble,
Creating euery bad a perfect beft
As faft as obiects to his beames affemble:
Oh tis the firft, tis flatry in my feeing,
And my great minde moft kingly drinkes it vp,
Mine eie well knowes what with his guft is greeing,
And to his pallat doth prepare the cup.
    If it be poifon'd, tis the leffer finne,
    That mine eye loues it and doth firft beginne.

115

THofe lines that I before haue writ doe lie,
Euen thofe that faid I could not loue you deerer,
Yet then my iudgement knew no reafon why,
My moft full flame fhould afterwards burne cleerer.
But reckening time, whofe milliond accidents
Creepe in twixt vowes, and change decrees of Kings,
Tan facred beautie, blunt the fharp'ft intents,
Diuert ftrong mindes to th' courfe of altring things:
Alas why fearing of times tiranie,

                     Might

Might I not then say now I loue you beſt,
When I was certaine ore in-certainty,
Crowning the preſent, doubting of the reſt:
   Loue is a Babe, then might I not ſay ſo
   To giue full growth to that which ſtill doth grow.

119

L Et me not to the marriage of true mindes
  Admit impediments, loue is not loue
Which alters when it alteration findes,
Or bends with the remouer to remoue.
O no, it is an euer fixed marke
That lookes on tempeſts and is neuer ſhaken;
It is the ſtar to euery wandring barke,
Whoſe worths vnknowne, although his higth be taken.
Lou's not Times foole, though roſie lips and cheeks
Within his bending ſickles compaſſe come,
Loue alters not with his breefe houres and weekes,
But beares it out euen to the edge of doome:
   If this be error and vpon me proued,
   I neuer writ, nor no man euer loued.

117

A Ccuſe me thus, that I haue ſcanted all,
  Wherein I ſhould your great deſerts repay,
Forgot vpon your deareſt loue to call,
Whereto al bonds do tie me day by day,
That I haue frequent binne with vnknown mindes,
And giuen to time your owne deare purchaſ'd right,
That I haue hoyſted ſaile to al the windes
Which ſhould tranſport me fartheſt from your ſight.
Booke both my wilfulneſſe and errors downe,
And on iuſt proofe ſurmiſe, accumilate,
Bring me within the leuel of your frowne,
But ſhoote not at me in your wakened hate:
   Since my appeale ſaies I did ſtriue to prooue
   The conſtancy and virtue of your loue

118

Like as to make our appetites more keene
With eager compounds we our pallat vrge,
As to preuent our malladies vnseene,
We sicken to shun sicknesse when we purge.
Euen so being full of your nere cloying sweetnesse,
To bitter sawces did I frame my feeding;
And sicke of wel-fare found a kind of meetnesse,
To be diseas'd ere that there was true needing.
Thus pollicie in loue t'anticipate
The ills that were, not grew to faults assured,
And brought to medicine a healthfull state
Which rancke of goodnesse would by ill be cured.
　But thence I learne and find the lesson true,
　Drugs poyson him that so fell sicke of you.

119

What potions haue I drunke of *Syren* teares
Distil'd from Lymbecks foule as hell within,
Applying feares to hopes, and hopes to feares,
Still loosing when I saw my selfe to win?
What wretched errors hath my heart committed,
Whilst it hath thought it selfe so blessed neuer?
How haue mine eies out of their Spheares bene fitted
In the distraction of this madding feuer?
O benefit of ill, now I find true
That better is, by euil still made better.
And ruin'd loue when it is built anew
Growes fairer then at first, more strong, far greater.
　So I returne rebukt to my content,
　And gaine by ills thrise more then I haue spent,

120

That you were once vnkind be-friends mee now,
And for that sorrow, which I then didde feele,
Needes must I vnder my transgression bow,
Vnlesse my Nerues were brasse or hammered steele.
For if you were by my vnkindnesse shaken

As

As I by yours , y'haue paſt a hell of Time,
And I a tyrant haue no leaſure taken
To waigh how once I ſuffered in **your crime.**
O that our night of wo might haue remembred
My deepeſt ſence,how hard true ſorrow hits,
And ſoone to you,as you to me then tendred
The humble ſalue,which wounded boſomes fits!
   But that your treſpaſſe now **becomes a fee,**
   Mine ranſoms yours,and yours muſt ranſome mee.

121

TIS better to be vile then vile eſteemed,
  When not to be,receiues reproach of being,
And the iuſt pleaſure loſt,which is ſo deemed,
Not by our feeling,but by others ſeeing.
For why ſhould others falſe adulterat eyes
Giue ſalutation to my ſportiue blood?
Or on my frailties why are frailer ſpies;
Which in their wils count bad what I think good?
Noe, I am that I am,and they that leuell
At my abuſes,reckon vp their owne,
I may be ſtraight though they them-ſelues be beuel
By their rancke thoughtes,my deedes muſt not be ſhown
   Vnleſſe this generall euill they maintaine,
   All men are bad and in their badneſſe raigne.

122.

THy guift,,thy tables,are within my braine
  Full characterd with laſting memory,
Which ſhall aboue that idle rancke remaine
Beyond all date euen to eternity.
Or at the leaſt,ſo **long** as braine and heart
Haue facukie by nature to ſubſiſt,
Til each to raz'd obliuion yeeld his part
Of thee,thy record neuer can be miſt:
That poore retention could not ſo much hold,
Nor need I tallies thy deare loue to skore,
Therefore to giue them from me was I bold,

To truft thofe tables that receaue thee more,
　　Fo keepe an adiunckt to remember thee,
　　Were to import forgetfulnefle in mee.

123

NO! Time, thou fhalt not boft that I doe change,
　　Thy pyramyds buylt vp with newer might
To me are nothing nouell,nothing ftrange,
They are but dreffings of a former fight:
Our dates are breefe,and therefor we admire,
What thou doft foyft vpon vs that is ould,
And rather make them borne to our defire,
Then thinke that we before haue heard them tould:
Thy regifters and thee I both defie,
Not wondring at the prefent,nor the paft,
For thy records,and what we fee doth lye,
Made more or les by thy continuall haft:
　　This I doe vow and this fhall euer be,
　　I will be true difpight thy fyeth and thee.

124

YF my deare loue were but the childe of ftate,
　　It might for fortunes bafterd be vnfathercd,
As fubiect to times loue,or to times hate,
Weeds among weeds,or flowers with flowers gatherd.
No it was buylded far from accident,
It fuffers not in fmilinge pomp,nor falls
Vnder the blow of thralled difcontent,
Whereto th'inuiting time our fafhion calls:
It feares not policy that *Heriticke*,
Which workes on leafes of fhort numbred howers,
But all alone ftands hugely pollitick,
That it nor growes with heat,nor drownes with fhowres,
　　To this I witnes call the foles of time,
　　Which die for goodnes,who haue liu'd for crime.

125

VVEr't ought to me I bore the canopy,
　　With my extern the outward honoring,

Or

Or layd great bafes for eternity,
Which proues more fhort then waft or ruining?
Haue I not feene dwellers on forme and fauor
Lofe all,and more by paying too **much rent**
For compound fweet;Forgoing fimple fauor,
Pittifull thriuors in their gazing fpent.
Noe,let me be obfequious in thy heart,
And take thou my oblacion,poore but free,
Which is not mixt with feconds,knows no art,
But mutuall render, onely me for thee.
    Hence,thou fubbornd *Informer*, a **trew foule**
    When moft impeacht,ftands leaft in thy **controule.**

126

OThou my louely Boy who in thy power,
  Doeft hould times fickle glaffe.his fickle,hower:
Who haft by wayning growne,and therein fhou'ft,
Thy louers withering,as thy fweet felfe grow'ft.
If Nature(foueraine mifteres ouer wrack)
As thou goeft onwards ftill will plucke thee backe,
She keepes thee to this purpofe,that her skill.
May time difgrace,and wretched mynuit kill.
Yet feare her O thou minnion of her pleafure,
She may detaine,but not ftill keepe her trefure!
Her *Audite*(though delayd)anfwer'd muft be,
And her *Quietus* is to render **thee.**

(   )
(   )

127

IN the ould age blacke was not counted faire,
  Or if it weare it bore not beauties name:
But now is blacke beauties fucceffiue heire,
And Beautie flanderd with a baftard fhame,
For fince each hand hath put on Natures power,
Fairing the foule with Arts faulfe borrow'd face,
Sweet beauty hath no name no holy boure,
But is prophan'd,if not liues in difgrace.

            Therefore

Therefore my Mifterffe eyes are Rauen blacke,
Her eyes fo futed,and they mourners feeme,
At fuch who not borne faire no beauty lack,
Slandring Creation with a falfe efteeme,
    Yet fo they mourne becomming of their woe,
    That euery toung faies beauty fhould looke fo.

128

HOw oft when thou my mufike mufike playft,
  Vpon that bleffed wood whofe motion founds
With thy fweet fingers when thou gently fwayft,
The wiry concord that mine eare coufounds,
Do I enuie thofe Iackes that nimble leape,
To kiffe the tender inward of thy hand,
Whilft my poore lips which fhould that haruest reape,
At the woods bouldnes by thee blufhing ftand.
To be fo tikled they would change their ftate,
And fituation with thofe dancing chips,
Ore whome their fingers walke with gentle gate,
Making dead wood more bleft then liuing lips,
    Since faufie Iackes fo happy are in this,
    Giue them their fingers,me thy lips to kiffe.

129

TH'expence of Spirit in a wafte of fhame
  Is luft in action,and till action , luft
Is periurd,murdrous,blouddy full of blame,
Sauage,extreame,rude,cruell,not to truft,
Inioyd no fooner but difpifed ftraight,
Paft reafon hunted, and no fooner had
Paft reafon hated as a fwollowed bayt,
On purpofe layd to make the taker mad.
Made In purfut and in poffeffion fo,
Had,hauing,and in queft,to haue extreame,
A bliffe in proofe and proud and very wo,
Before a ioy propofd behind a dreame,
    All this the world well knowes yet none knowes well,
    To fhun the heauen that leads men to this hell.

                          My

130

MY Miſtres eyes are nothing like the Sunne,
Currall is farre more red, then her lips red,
If ſnow be white why then her breſts are dun:
If haires be wiers, black wiers grow on her head:
I haue ſcene Roſes damaskt, red and white,
But no ſuch Roſes ſee I in her checkes,
And in ſome perfumes is there more delight,
Then in the breath that from my Miſtres reckes.
I loue to heare her ſpeake, yet well I know,
That Muſicke hath a farre more pleaſing ſound:
I graunt I neuer ſaw a goddeſſe goe,
My Miſtres when ſhee walkes treads on the ground.
　　And yet by heauen I thinke my loue as rare,
　　As any ſhe beli'd with falſe compare.

131

THou art as tiranous, ſo as thou art,
As thoſe whoſe beauties proudly make them cruell;
For well thou know'ſt to my deare doting hart
Thou art the faireſt and moſt precious Iewell.
Yet in good faith ſome ſay that thee behold,
Thy face hath not the power to make loue grone;
To ſay they erre, I dare not be ſo bold,
Although I ſweare it to my ſelfe alone.
And to be ſure that is not falſe I ſweare
A thouſand grones but thinking on thy face,
One on anothers necke do witneſſe beare
Thy blacke is faireſt in my iudgements place.
　　In nothing art thou blacke ſaue in thy deeds,
　　And thence this ſlaunder as I thinke proceeds.

132

THine eies I loue, and they as pittying me,
Knowing thy heart torment me with diſdaine,
Haue put on black, and louing mourners bee,
Looking with pretty ruth vpon my paine.

And

And truly not the morning Sun of Heauen
Better becomes the gray cheeks of th'Eaſt
Nor that full Starre that vſhers in the Eauen
Doth halfe that glory to the ſober Weſt
As thoſe two morning eyes become thy face:
O let it then as well beſeeme thy heart
To mourne for me ſince mourning doth thee grace,
And ſute thy pitty like in euery part.
    Then will I ſweare beauty her ſelfe is blacke,
    And all they foule that thy complexion lacke.

133

BEſhrew that heart that makes my heart to groane
  For that deepe wound it giues my friend and me;
I'ſt not ynough to torture me alone,
But ſlaue to ſlauery my ſweet'ſt friend muſt be.
Me from my ſelfe thy cruell eye hath taken,
And my next ſelfe thou harder haſt ingroſſed,
Of him, my ſelfe, and thee I am forſaken,
A torment thrice three-fold thus to be croſſed:
Priſon my heart in thy ſteele boſomes warde,
But then my friends heart let my poore heart bale,
Who ere keepes me, let my heart be his garde,
Thou canſt not then vſe rigor in my Iaile.
    And yet thou wilt, for I being pent in thee,
    Perforce am thine and all that is in me.

134

SO now I haue confeſt that he is thine,
  And I my ſelfe am morgag'd to thy will,
My ſelfe Ile forfeit, ſo that other mine,
Thou wilt reſtore to be my comfort ſtill:
But thou wilt not, nor he will not be free,
For thou art couetous, and he is kinde,
He learnd but ſuretie-like to write for me,
Vnder that bond that him as faſt doth binde.
The ſtatute of thy beauty thou wilt take,
Thou vſurer that put'ſt forth all to vſe,

And

And sue a friend,came debter for my sake,
So him I loose through my vnkinde abuse.
 Him haue I lost, thou hast both him and me,
 He paies the whole,and yet am I not free.

135

WHo euer hath her wish,thou hast thy *Will*,
 And *Will* too boote,and *Will* in ouer-plus,
More then enough am I that vexe thee still,
To thy sweet will making addition thus.
Wilt thou whose will is large and spatious,
Not once vouchsafe to hide my will in thine,
Shall will in others seeme right gracious,
And in my will no faire acceptance shine:
The sea all water,yet receiues raine still,
And in aboundance addeth to his store,
So thou beeing rich in *Will* adde to thy *Will*,
One will of mine to make thy large *Will* more.
 Let no vnkinde,no faire beseechers kill,
 Thinke all but one,and me in that one *Will*.

136

IF thy soule check thee that I come so neere,
Sweare to thy blind soule that I was thy *Will*,
And will thy soule knowes is admitted there,
Thus farre for loue, my loue-sute sweet fullfill.
Will, will fulfill the treasure of thy loue,
I fill it full with wils,and my will one,
In things of great receit with ease we prooue,
Among a number one is reckon'd none.
Then in the number let me passe vntold,
Though in thy stores account I one must be,
For nothing hold me,so it please thee hold,
That nothing me,a some-thing sweet to thee.
 Make but my name thy loue,and loue that still,
 And then thou louest me for my name is *Will*.

137

THou blinde foole loue,what doost thou to mine eyes,

I   That

That they behold and fee not what they fee :
They know what beautie is,fee where it lyes,
Yet what the beft is,take the worft to be.
If eyes corrupt by ouer-partiall lookes,
Be anchord in the baye where all men ride,
Why of eyes falfehood haft thou forged hookes,
Whereto the iudgement of my heart is tide ?
Why fhould my heart thinke that a feuerall plot,
Which my heart knowes the wide worlds common place?
Or mine eyes feeing this,fay this is not
To put faire truth vpon fo foule a face,
   In things right true my heart and eyes haue erred,
   And to this falfe plague are they now tranfferred.

138

*W*Hen my loue fweares that fhe is made of truth,
  I do beleeue her though I know fhe lyes,
That fhe might thinke me fome vntuterd youth,
Vnlearned in the worlds falfe fubtilties.
Thus vainely thinking that fhe thinkes me young,
Although fhe knowes my dayes are paft the beft,
Simply I credit her falfe fpeaking tongue,
On both fides thus is fimple truth fuppreft :
But wherefore fayes fhe not fhe is vniuft ?
And wherefore fay not I that I am old ?
O loues beft habit is in feeming truft,
And age in loue,loues not t'haue yeares told.
   Therefore I lye with her,and fhe with me,
   And in our faults by lyes we flattered be.

139

O Call not me to iuftifie the wrong,
  That thy vnkindneffe layes vpon my heart,
Wound me not with thine eye but with thy toung,
Vfe power with power,and flay me not by Art,
Tell me thou lou'ft elfe-where;but in my fight,
Deare heart forbeare to glance thine eye afide,
What needft thou wound with cunning when thy might

Is

Is more then my ore-prest defence can bide?
Let me excuse thee, ah my loue well knowes,
Her prettie lookes haue beene mine enemies,
And therefore from my face she turnes my foes,
That they else-where might dart their iniuries :
   Yet do not so, but since I am neere slaine,
   Kill me out-right with lookes, and rid my paine.

140

BE wise as thou art cruell, do not presse
  My toung-tide patience with too much disdaine :
Least sorrow lend me words and words expresse,
The manner of my pittie wanting paine.
If I might teach thee witte better it weare,
Though not to loue, yet loue to tell me so,
As testie sick-men when their deaths be neere,
No newes but health from their Phisitions know.
For if I should dispaire I should grow madde,
And in my madnesse might speake ill of thee,
Now this ill wresting world is growne so bad,
Madde slanderers by madde eares beleeued be.
   That I may not be so, nor thou be lyde,   (wide.
   Beare thine eyes straight, though thy proud heart goe

141

IN faith I doe not loue thee with mine eyes,
 For they in thee a thousand errors note,
But 'tis my heart that loues what they dispise,
Who in dispight of view is pleas'd to dote.
Nor are mine eares with thy toungs tune delighted,
Nor tender feeling to base touches prone,
Nor taste, nor smell, desire to be inuited
To any sensuall feast with thee alone :
But my fiue wits, nor my fiue sences can
Diswade one foolish heart from seruing thee,
Who leaues vnswai'd the likenesse of a man,
Thy proud hearts slaue and vassall wretch to be :
   Onely my plague thus farre I count my gaine,
   That she that makes me sinne, awards me paine.

142

LOue is my finne, and thy deare vertue hate,
Hate of my finne, grounded on finfull louing,
O but with mine, compare thou thine owne ftate,
And thou fhalt finde it merrits not reproouing,
Or if it do, not from thofe lips of thine,
That haue prophan'd their fcarlet ornaments,
And feald falfe bonds of loue as oft as mine,
Robd others beds reuenues of their rents.
Be it lawfull I loue thee as thou lou'ft thofe,
Whome thine eyes wooe as mine importune thee,
Roote pittie in thy heart that when it growes,
Thy pitty may deferue to pittied bee.
　　If thou dooft feeke to haue what thou dooft hide,
　　By felfe example mai'ft thou be denide.

143

LOe as a carefull hufwife runnes to catch,
One of her fethered creatures broake away,
Sets downe her babe and makes all fwift difpatch
In purfuit of the thing fhe would haue ftay:
Whilft her neglected child holds her in chace,
Cries to catch her whofe bufie care is bent,
To follow that which flies before her face:
Not prizing her poore infants difcontent;
So runft thou after that which flies from thee,
Whilft I thy babe chace thee a farre behind,
But if thou catch thy hope turne back to me:
And play the mothers part kiffe me, be kind.
　　So will I pray that thou maift haue thy *Will*,
　　If thou turne back and my loude crying ftill.

144

TWo loues I haue of comfort and difpaire,
Which like two fpirits do fugieft me ftill,
The better angell is a man right faire:
The worfer fpirit a woman collour'd ill.
To win me foone to hell my femall euill,

Tempteth

Tempteth my better angel from my fight,
And would corrupt my faint to be a diuel:
Wooing his purity with her fowle pride.
And whether that my angel be turn'd finde,
Sufpect I may, yet not directly tell,
But being both from me both to each friend,
I geffe one angel in an others hel.
   Yet this fhal I nere know but liue in doubt,
   Till my bad angel fire my good one out.

145

THofe lips that Loues owne hand did make,
   Breath'd forth the found that faid I hate,
To me that languifh: for her fake:
But when fhe faw my wofull ftate,
Straight in her heart did mercie come,
Chiding that tongue that euer fweet,
Was vfde in giuing gentle dome:
And tought it thus a new to greete:
I hate fhe alterd with an end,
That follow'd it as gentle day,
Doth follow night who like a fiend
From heauen to hell is flowne away.
   I hate, from hate away fhe threw,
   And fau'd my life faying not you.

146

POore foule the center of my finfull earth,
   My finfull earth thefe rebbell powres that thee array,
Why doft thou pine within and fuffer dearth,
Painting thy outward walls fo coftie gay?
Why fo large coft hauing fo fhort a leafe,
Doft thou vpon thy fading manfion fpend?
Shall wormes inheritors of this exceffe,
Eate vp thy charge? is this thy bodies end?
Then foule liue thou vpon thy feruants loffe,
And let that pine to aggrauat thy ftore;
Buy tearmes diuine in felling houres of droffe:

       Within

Within be fed, without be rich no more,
  So shalt thou feed on death,that feeds on men,
  And death once dead,ther's no more dying then.

147

MY loue is as a feauer longing still,
  For that which longer nurseth the disease,
Feeding on that which doth preserue the ill,
Th'vncertaine sicklie appetite to please:
My reason the Phisition to my loue,
Angry that his prescriptions are not kept
Hath left me,and I desperate now approoue,
Desire is death,which Phisick did except.
Past cure I am,now Reason is past care,
And frantick madde with euer-more vnrest,
My thoughts and my discourse as mad mens are,
At randon from the truth vainely exprest.
  For I haue sworne thee faire,and thought thee bright,
  Who art as black as hell,as darke as night.

148

O Me ! what eyes hath loue put in my head,
  Which haue no correspondence with true sight,
Or if they haue,where is my iudgment fled,
That censures falsely what they see aright ?
If that be faire whereon my false eyes dote,
What meanes the world to say it is not so?
If it be not,then loue doth well denote,
Loues eye is not so true as all mens:no,
How can it ? O how can loues eye be true,
That is so vext with watching and with teares?
No maruaile then though I mistake my view,
The sunne it selfe sees not, till heauen cleeres.
  O cunning loue,with teares thou keep'st me blinde,
  Least eyes well seeing thy foule faults should finde.

149

CAnst thou O cruell,say I loue thee not,
  When I against my selfe with thee pertake:

Doe

Doe I not thinke on thee when I forgot
Am of my selfe, all tirant for thy fake?
Who hateth thee that I doe call my friend,
On whom froun'ft thou that I doe faune vpon,
Nay if thou lowrft on me doe I not fpend
Reuenge vpon my felfe with prefent mone?
What merrit do I in my felfe refpect,
That is fo proude thy feruice to difpife,
When all my beft doth worfhip thy defect,
Commanded by the motion of thine eyes.
   But loue hate on for now I know thy minde,
   Thofe that can fee thou lou'ft,and I am blind.

150

OH from what powre haft thou this powrefull might,
  VVith infufficiency my heart to fway,
To make me giue the lie to my true fight,
And fwere that brightneffe doth not grace the day?
Whence haft thou this becomming of things il,
That in the very refufe of thy deeds,
There is fuch ftrength and warrantie of skill,
That in my minde thy worft all beft exceeds?
Who taught thee how to make me loue thee more,
The more I heare and fee iuft caufe of hate,
Oh though I loue what others doe abhor,
VVith others thou fhould!t not abhor my ftate.
   If thy vnworthineffe raifd loue in me,
   More worthy I to be belou'd of thee.

151

LOue is too young to know what confcience is,
  Yet who knowes not confcience is borne of loue,
Then gentle cheater vrge not my amiffe,
Leaft guilty of my faults thy fweet felfe proue.
For thou betraying me, I doe betray
My nobler part to my grofe bodies treafon,
My foule doth tell my body that he may,
Triumph in loue,flefh ftaies no farther reafon,

                  But

But ryſing at thy name doth point out thee,
As his triumphant prize,proud of this pride,
He is contented thy poore drudge to be
To ſtand in thy affaires,fall by thy ſide.
    No want of conſcience hold it that I call,
    Her loue,for whoſe deare loue I riſe and fall.

152

IN louing thee thou know'ſt I am forſworne,
But thou art twice forſworne to me loue ſwearing,
In act thy bed-vow broake and new faith torne,
In vowing new hate after new loue bearing:
But why of two othes breach doe I accuſe thee,
When I breake twenty:I am periur'd moſt,
For all my vowes are othes but to miſuſe thee:
And all my honeſt faith in thee is loſt.
For I haue ſworne deepe othes of thy deepe kindneſſe:
Othes of thy loue,thy truth,thy conſtancie,
And to inlighten thee gaue eyes to blindneſſe,
Or made them ſwere againſt the thing they ſee.
    For I haue ſworne thee faire:more periurde eye,
    To ſwere againſt the truth ſo foule a lie.

153

CVpid laid by his brand and fell a ſleepe,
A maide of *Dyans* this aduantage found,
And his loue-kindling fire did quickly ſteepe
In a could vallie-fountaine of that ground:
Which borrowd from this holie fire of loue,
A dateleſſe liuely heat ſtill to indure,
And grew a ſeething bath which yet men proue,
Againſt ſtrang malladies a ſoueraigne cure:
But at my miſtres eie loues brand new fired,
The boy for triall needes would touch my breſt,
I ſick withall the helpe of bath deſired,
And thether hied a ſad diſtemperd gueſt.
    But found no cure,the bath for my helpe lies,
    Where *Cupid* got new fire;my miſtres eye.

THe little Loue-God lying once a fleepe,
Laid by his fide his heart inflaming brand,
Whilft many Nymphes that vou'd chaft life to keep.
Came tripping by, but in her maiden hand,
The fayreft votary tooke vp that fire,
Which many Legions of true hearts had warm'd,
And fo the Generall of hot defire,
Was fleeping by a Virgin hand difarm'd.
This brand fhe quenched in a coole Well by,
Which from loues fire tooke heat perpetuall,
Growing a bath and healthfull remedy,
For men difeafd, but I my Miftriffe thrall,
   Came there for cure and this by that I proue,
   Loues fire heates water, water cooles not loue.

FINIS.

K   A

A Louers complaint.

BY

WILLIAM SHAKE-SPEARE.

FRom off a hill whofe concaue wombe reworded,
  A plaintfull ftory from a fiftring vale
My fpirrits t'attend this doble voyce accorded,
And downe I laid to lift the fad tun'd tale,
Ere long efpied a fickle maid full pale
Tearing of papers breaking rings a twaine,
Storming her world with forrowes, wind and raine.

Vpon her head a plattid hiue of ftraw,
Which fortified her vifage from the Sunne,
Whereon the thought might thinke fometime it faw
The carkas of a beauty fpent and donne,
Time had not fithed all that youth begun,
Nor youth all quit, but fpight of heauens fell rage,
Some beauty peept, through lettice of fear'd age.

Oft did fhe heaue her Napkin to her eyne,
Which on it had conceited charecters:
Laundring the filken figures in the brine,
That feafoned woe had pelleted in teares,
And often reading what contents it beares:
As often fhriking vndiftinguifht wo,
In clamours of all fize both high and low.

Some-times her leueld eyes their carriage ride,
As they did battry to the fpheres intend:
Sometime diuerted their poore balls are tide,
To th'orbed earth; fometimes they do extend,
Their view right on, anon their gafes lend,

To

To euery place at once and no where fixt,
The mind and fight diftractedly commixt.

Her haire nor loofe nor ti'd in formall plat,
Proclaimd in her a carelefse hand of pride;
For fome vntuck'd defcended her fheu'd hat,
Hanging her pale and pined cheeke befide,
Some in her threeden fillet ftill did bide,
And trew to bondage would not breake from thence,
Though flackly braided in loofe negligence.

A thoufand fauours from a maund **fhe drew,**
Of amber chriftall and of bedded **Iet,**
Which one by one fhe in **a riuer threw,**
Vpon whofe weeping margent fhe was fet,
Like vfery applying wet to wet,
Or Monarches hands that lets not bounty fall,
Where want cries fome; but where excefse begs all.

Of folded fchedulls had fhe many a one,
Which fhe peruf'd, fighd, tore and gaue the flud,
Crackt many a ring of Pofied gold and bone,
Bidding them find their Sepulchers in mud,
Found yet mo letters fadly pend in blood,
With fleided filke, feate and **affectedly**
Enfwath'd and fcald to curious fecrecy.

Thefe often bath'd fhe in her fluxiue eies,
And often kift, and often gaue to teare,
Cried O falfe blood thou regifter of lies,
What vnapproued witnes dooft thou beare!
Inke would haue feem'd more blacke and damned heare!
This faid in top of rage the lines fhe rents,
Big difcontent, fo breaking their contents.

A reuerend man that graz'd his cattell ny,

Some.

Sometime a blusterer that the rustle knew
Of Court of Cittie, and had let go by
The swiftest houres obserued as they flew,
Towards this afflicted fancy fastly drew:
And priuiledg'd by age desires to know
In breefe the grounds and motiues of her wo.

So slides he downe vppon his greyned bat;
And comely distant sits he by her side,
When hee againe desires her, being satte,
Her greeuance with his hearing to deuide·
If that from him there may be ought applied
Which may her suffering extasie asswage
Tis promist in the charitie of age.

Father she saies, though in mee you behold
The iniury of many a blasting houre;
Let it not tell your Iudgement I am old,
Not age, but sorrow, ouer me hath power;
I might as yet haue bene a spreading flower
Fresh to my selfe, if I had selfe applyed
Loue to my selfe, and to no Loue beside.

But wo is mee, too early I atttended
A youthfull suit it was to gaine my grace;
O one by natures outwards so commended,
That maidens eyes stucke ouer all his face,
Loue lackt a dwelling and made him her place.
And when in his faire parts shee didde abide,
Shee was new lodg'd and newly Deified.

His browny locks did hang in crooked curles,
And euery light occasion of the wind
Vpon his lippes their silken parcels hurles,
Whats sweet to do, to do wil aptly find,
Each eye that saw him did inchaunt the minde:

For on his vifage was in little drawne,
What largeneffe thinkes in parradife was fawne.

Smal fhew of man was yet vpon his chinne,
His phenix downe began but to appeare
Like vnfhorne veluet,on that termleffe skin
Whofe bare out-brag'd the web it feem'd to were.
Yet fhewed his vifage by that coft more deare,
And nice affections wauering ftood in doubt
If beft were as it was,or beft without.

His qualities were beautious as his forme,
For maiden tongu'd he was and thereof free;
Yet if men mou'd him,was he fuch a ftorme
As oft twixt May and Aprill is to fee,
When windes breath fweet,vnruly though they bee.
His rudeneffe fo with his authoriz'd youth,
Did liuery falfeneffe in a pride of truth,

Wel could hee ride, and often men would fay
That horfe his mettell from his rider takes
Proud of fubiection,noble by the fwaie,   (makes
What rounds,what bounds,what courfe what ftop he
And controuerfie hence a queftion takes,
Whether the horfe by him became his deed,
Or he his mannad'g , by'th wel doing Steed.

But quickly on this fide the verdict went,
His reall habitude gaue life and grace
To appertainings and to ornament,
Accomplifht in him-felfe not in his cafe:
All ayds them-felues made fairer by their place,
Can for addicions,yet their purpof'd trimme
Peec'd not his grace but were al grac'd by him. !

So on the tip of his fubduing tongue

All kinde of arguments and queſtion deepe,
Al replication prompt, and reaſon ſtrong
For his aduantage ſtill did wake and ſleep,
To make the weeper laugh, the laugher weepe:
He hadthe dialect and different skil,
Catching al paſſions in his craft of will.

That hee didde in the general boſome raigne
Of young, of old, and ſexes both inchanted.
To dwel with him in thoughts, or to remaine
In perſonal duty, following where he haunted,
Conſent's bewitcht, ere he deſire haue granted,
And dialogu'd for him what he would ſay,
Askt their own wils and made their wils obey.

Many there were that did his picture gette
To ſerue their eies, and in it put their mind,
Like fooles that in th' imagination ſet
The goodly obiects which abroad they find
Of lands and manſions, theirs in thought aſſign'd,
And labouring in moe pleaſures to beſtow them,
Then the true gouty Land-lord which doth owe them.

So many haue that neuer toucht his hand
Sweetly ſuppoſ'd them miſtreſſe of his heart:
My wofull ſelfe that did in freedome ſtand,
And was my owne fee ſimple (not in part)
What with his art in youth and youth in art
Threw my affections in his charmed power,
Reſeru'd the ſtalke and gaue him al my flower.

Yet did I not as ſome my equals did
Demaund of him, nor being deſired yeelded,
Finding my ſelfe in honour ſo forbidde,
With ſafeſt diſtance I mine honour ſheelded,
Experience for me many bulwarkes builded

Of proofs new bleeding which remaind the foile
Of this false Iewell, and his amorous spoile.

But ah who euer shun'd by precedent,
The destin'd ill she must her selfe assay,
Or forc'd examples gainst her owne content
To put the by-past perrils in her way?
Counsaile may stop a while what will not stay:
For when we rage, aduise is often seene
By blunting vs to make our wits more keene.

Nor giues it satisfaction to our blood,
That wee must curbe it vppon others proofe,
To be forbod the sweets that seemes so good,
For feare of harmes that preach in our behoofe;
O appetite from iudgement stand aloofe!
The one a pallate hath that needs will taste,
Though reason weepe and cry it is thy last.

For further I could say this mans vntrue,
And knew the patternes of his foule beguiling,
Heard where his plants in others Orchards grew,
Saw how deceits were guilded in his smiling,
Knew vowes, wer e euer brokers to defiling,
Thought Characters and words meerly but art,
And bastards of his foule adulterat heart.

And long vpon these termes I held my Citty,
Till thus hee gan besiege me : Gentle maid
Haue of my suffering youth some feeling pitty
And be not of my holy vowes affraid,
Thats to ye sworne to none was euer said,
For feasts of loue I haue bene call'd vnto
Till now did nere inuite nor neuer vovv.

All my offences that abroad you see

Are

Are errors of the blood none of the mind?
Loue made them not, with acture they may be,
Where neither Party'is nor trew nor kind,
They sought their shame that so their shame did find,
And so much lesse of shame in me remaines,
By how much of me their reproch containes,

Among the many that mine eyes haue seene,
Not one whose flame my hart so much as warmed,
Or my affection put to th'smallest teene,
Or any of my leisures euer Charmed,
Harme haue I done to them but nere was harmed,
Kept hearts in liueries, but mine owne was free,
And raignd commaunding in his monarchy.

Looke heare what tributes wounded fancies sent me,
Of palyd pearles and rubies red as blood:
Figuring that they their passions likewise lent me
Of greefe and blushes, aptly vnderstood
In bloodlesse white, and the encrimson'd mood,
Effects of terror and deare modesty,
Encampt in hearts but fighting outwardly.

And Lo behold these tallents of their heir,
With twisted mettle amorously empleacht
I haue receau'd from many a seueral faire,
Their kind acceptance, wepingly beseecht,
With th'annexions of faire gems inricht,
And deepe brain'd sonnets that did amplifie
Each stones deare Nature, worth and quallity.

The Diamond? why twas beautifull and hard,
Whereto his inuis'd properties did tend,
The deepe greene Emrald in whose fresh regard,
Weake sights their sickly radience do amend.
The heauen hewd Saphir and the Opall blend

With

With obiects manyfold ; each feuerall ftone,
With wit well blazond fmil'd or made fome mone.

Lo all thefe trophies of affections hot,
Of penfiu'd and fubdew'd defires the tender,
Nature hath chargd me that I hoord them not,
But yeeld them vp where I my felfe muft render:
That is to you my origin and ender :
For thefe of force muft your oblations be,
Since I their Aulter, you en patrone me.

Oh then aduance(of yours)that phrafeles hand,
Whofe white weighes downe the airy fcale of praife,
Take all thefe fimilies to your owne command,
Hollowed with fighes that burning lunges did raife:
What me your minifter for you obaies
Workes vnder you,and to your audit comes
Their diftract parcells,in combined fummes.

Lo this deuice was fent me from a Nun,
Or Sifter fanctified of holieft note,
Which late her noble fuit in court did fhun,
Whofe rareft hauings made the bloffoms dote,
For fhe was fought by fpirits of ritcheft cote,
But kept cold diftance,and did thence remoue,
To fpend her liuing in eternall loue.

But oh my fweet what labour ift to leaue,
The thing we haue not,maftring what not ftriues,
Playing the Place which did no forme receiue,
Playing patient fports in vnconftraind giues,
She that her fame fo to her felfe contriues,
The fcarres of battaile fcapeth by the flight,
And makes her abfence valiant,not her might.

Oh pardon me in that my boaft is true,

L

The accident which brought me to her eie,
Vpon the moment did her force subdewe,
And now she would the caged cloister flie:
Religious loue put out religions eye:
Not to be tempted would she be enur'd,
And now to tempt all liberty procure.

How mightie then you are, Oh heare me tell,
The broken bosoms that to me belong,
Haue emptied all their fountaines in my well:
And mine I powre your Ocean all amonge:
I strong ore them and you ore me being strong,
Must for your victorie vs all congest,
As compound loue to phisick your cold brest.

My parts had powre to charme a sacred Sunne,
Who disciplin'd I dieted in grace,
Beleeu'd her eies, when they t' assaile begun,
All vowes and consecrations giuing place:
O most potentiall loue, vowe, bond, nor space
In thee hath neither sting, knot, nor confine
For thou art all and all things els are thine.

When thou impressest what are precepts worth
Of stale example? when thou wilt inflame,
How coldly those impediments stand forth
Of wealth of filliall feare, lawe, kindred fame,   (shame
Loues armes are peace, gainst rule, gainst sence, gainst
And sweetens in the suffring pangues it beares,
The *Alloes* of all forces, shockes and feares.

Now all these hearts that doe on mine depend,
Feeling it breake, with bleeding groanes they pine,
And supplicant their sighes to you extend
To leaue the battrie that you make gainst mine,
Lending soft audience, to my sweet designe,

                                                                And

And credent soule,to that strong bonded oth,
That shall preferre and vndertake my troth.

This said,his watrie eies he did dismount,
Whose sightes till then were leaueld on my face,
Each cheeke a riuer running from a sount,
With brynish currant downe-ward flowed a pace:
Oh how the channell to the streame gaue grace!
Who glaz'd with Christall gate the glowing Roses,
That flame through water which their hew incloses,

Oh father,what a hell of witch-craft lies,
In the small orb of one perticular teare?
But with the invndation of the eies:
What rocky heart to water will not weare?
What brest so cold that is not warmed heare,
Or cleft effect,cold modesty hot wrath:
Both fire from hence,and chill extincture hath.

For loe his passion but an art of craft,
Euen there resolu'd my reason into teares,
There my white stole of chastity I daft,
Shooke off my sober gardes,and ciuill feares,
Appeare to him as he to me appeares:
All melting,though our drops this diffrence bore,
His poison'd me,and mine did him restore.

In him a plenitude of subtle matter,
Applied to Cautills,all straing formes receiues,
Of burning blushes,or of weeping water,
Or sounding palenesse: and he takes and leaues,
In eithers aptnesse as it best deceiue:
To blush at speeches ranck,to weepe at woes
Or to turne white and sound at tragick showes.

That not a heart which in his leuell came,

Could

Cou'd scape the haile of his all hurting ayme,
Shewing faire Nature is both kinde and tame:
And vaild in them did winne whom he would maime,
Against the thing he sought, he would exclaime,
When he most burnt in hart-wisht luxurie,
He preacht pure maide, and praisd cold chastitie.

Thus meerely with the garment of a grace,
The naked and concealed feind he couerd,
That th'vnexperient gaue the tempter place,
Which like a Cherubin aboue them houerd,
Who young and simple would not be so louerd.
Aye me I fell, and yet do question make,
What I should doe againe for such a sake.

O that infected moysture of his eye,
O that false fire which in his cheeke so glowd:
O that forc'd thunder from his heart did flye,
O that sad breath his spungie lungs bestowed,
O all that borrowed motion seeming owed,
Would yet againe betray the fore-betrayed,
And new peruert a reconciled Maide,

FINIS.

www.ingramcontent.com/pod-product-compliance
Lightning Source LLC
Chambersburg PA
CBHW032353020726
47499CB00008B/2728